Coming of Age

Coming of Age

Valerie Mendes

SIMON &
SCHUSTER

SIMON &
SCHUSTER

First published in Great Britain by Simon & Schuster UK Ltd, 2003
A Viacom company

Copyright © 2003 Valerie Mendes
Cover illustration copyright © 2003 Ian Winstanley

Simon & Schuster UK Ltd
Africa House, 64-78 Kingsway, London WC2B 6AH

A CIP catalogue record for this book is available from the British Library

ISBN 0 689 83716 X

1 3 5 7 9 10 8 6 4 2

Printed and bound in Finland by WS Bookwell

For Stephen Cole,
A brilliant editor and a beloved friend

Acknowledgements

My gratitude and love go to Sam Mendes for his generous financial support and unwavering encouragement, without which writing this novel would have been utterly impossible; his continual right-hand woman, Tara B. Cook, for masterminding my trip to Italy – and only she knows how much more; Janine Gray for her sweetness and light on all matters personal and domestic; Maurizio Ammazzini, Carlo Soldani and the miraculously restored White Cat at the Villa San Michele, Fiesole, Florence, for their immaculate help and hospitality; Pamela Cleaver and Maggie Hamand for their constructive reading of early synopses; all the staff of Grayshott Hall, Hindhead; my Grayshott drivers – Jean, Tom and Michael – who made possible many research expeditions; Mary Peters of Mayfair Farm and Riding Stables for her knowledge, experience and caring empire; and Major Jeremy Whitaker and his family in the Land of Nod for taking the time and trouble to read the final draft.

My thanks also go to the professionalism, enthusiasm and expertise of the Simon & Schuster Children's Books publishing team, without whom I should undoubtedly still be sitting in the slush pile of some sleepy office; to our copy-editor Lesley Levene; and to Ian Winstanley for a stunning jacket illustration.

Last, I need to thank Robert McKee for his outstanding story seminars, which guide, inspire and live on.

1

Amy grips her father's hand, as hard as her frozen fingers will allow.

Dad's hand feels plump and hot and sweaty. Amy looks up at him, noticing for the first time the flutter of grey eating into the thick brown waves of hair above his ears.

I want to be glued to Dad for ever, so he'll never leave me. Wherever I go, he'll be close to me, so nothing can happen to him. Nothing can take him away from me. Or, if it does, I can go with him.

The January wind bites across the Surrey sky over the graveyard, drifting into Amy's face a cold sleet that clings to her lips and eyelashes. When she blinks, pale drops splash to her cheeks, her neat, shining chestnut plaits which flick forward over her shoulders, down on to her smart navy Sunday-best coat.

The coffin bumps and rasps against the sides of the hole, settles on the earth with a dull thud. Sleet finds the wooden surface and licks it shiny wet.

It's Mum inside that box. Her eyes are closed, her neck is white with those spidery-thin lines. Her hair, all her lovely dark-red hair, is curling on her shoulders. I wonder what she's wearing, what they've put her in.

Amy bends forward so she can see past Dad to her brother, Julian. He's thirteen, four years older than her, and she adores him. He stands stiffly by Dad's side, his head bent, his hands thrust into his coat pockets. He'd returned to Grayshott yesterday from his Oxford boarding school, driven by one of the masters, a tall, thin man with a red nose and embarrassed eyes who hovered in the hall and then vanished back to his car with obvious relief.

Julian had looked pale, dry-eyed. He hugged Amy, said, "Hi, sis," and stared wretchedly into her silent face. Then he ran up to his room and shut the door. Amy followed him and paused outside. She knocked, but got no answer. She hadn't dared go in. Instead she ran into her bedroom, stood at the window looking out at the garden. Mum's garden, the one she'd designed and made, cared for so lovingly, now bleak and winter-wet.

Dad came home from the surgery, rushed up to see Julian. Their voices mumbled on for ages behind the door.

Now a strange sound breaks from her father's mouth, a kind of cry, but choked and muffled, as if it had escaped without permission. He clears his throat.

"Lauren, my love," he says.

Amy blinks and looks around the graveyard. For a wild moment she thinks she can see the dead rising from their graves. Their faces are pale, their clothes drab, their hair flutters in the wind. One of them, a woman dressed in black, carries a baby in her arms. Then the creatures sigh. They dissolve once again into the ground.

Frightened, Amy grips Dad's hand tighter still. She tugs at it, makes him look down at her. His eyes, pink around the edges, grey with tiredness, stare at her, but they don't see her. Sunk in misery, they look back into his own head.

Amy opens her mouth. She wants to say, "Don't cry, Dad." She tries to say, "I promise I'll remember what happened. One morning, soon, I'll wake up and I'll be able to speak again. My voice will sound just the same as before and I'll tell you what happened, because every minute will have come back to me."

The words ring in her head. They climb up her throat, but something swallows them before they reach her mouth.

Dad tries to smile at her and Amy tries to speak.

Both of them fail.

"Poor little mite."

Amy hears the whisperings about her begin as the scrapes of earth crunch on the coffin. Rooks cling and caw insistently among the giant firs; the mourners huddle into groups against the wind.

"She's only nine years old, you know . . . Terrible thing to witness . . . She ran for help. Got off her pony and stumbled across Ludshott Common. Flung herself at the door of the nearest house, fainted dead away."

"How terrible . . . "

"When she came round, she couldn't say a word. Just shook her head and pointed to the Common, crying as if her heart would break but not making a sound. Her dog, Tyler, was with her, barking fit to burst. They followed him and found Lauren lying on the path . . . Nothing they could do to help . . . too late for anything."

"And Amy still can't —"

"No, not a word. Hasn't said a word since that dreadful day."

"Where was Dr Grant at the time?"

"Dreadfully ill. Flu epidemic all winter. Hit the village hard. He's such a lovely man, do anything for anybody — home visits, weekends . . . "

Restlessly, the mourners begin to shift away from the grave, down the tarmac path shot through with patches of ice and sharp yellow moss, towards Terra Firma, the Grant family's house.

Amy feels hands stroking her shoulders. Aunt Charlotte

bends to kiss her. She's older than Mum and not a bit like her – very thin, with beautiful clothes. "Come on, my darling. Let's get back into the warm."

Amy lets go of Dad. She buries her face in the softness of Aunt Charlotte's coat. It smells of sugared almonds. Wisps of mohair find their way into her mouth.

Back at Terra Firma, the hall fills with damp coats and the spikes of dripping umbrellas. Tyler skitters up and down, yapping excitedly at the strangers who throng the living room. Bottles chink, glasses fill, sherry scents the air.

Someone rings a spoon against a glass. The voices hush.

"I want to thank everyone for making time to come to Lauren's funeral and for being here with us this afternoon." Dr William Grant's voice falters. "Lauren and I were childhood sweethearts. She was my wife and dearly beloved partner for fifteen years . . . For me, she will never die. And I know that many of you here, her good friends and neighbours, whose gardens she designed and helped create, will always have those to remember her by. I hope that by tending them in future, you too will be able to keep her memory alive."

His voice almost breaks.

"I don't know what I'm going to do without her."

Murmurs of sympathy fill the room.

"But —" Dr Grant takes a deep breath and perseveres — "Amy and Julian are by my side, and Lauren's dear sister, Charlotte, will stay with us until we are strong again."

He smiles at Charlotte through tearful eyes.

"And of course my job as your GP will continue. In fact —" he swallows — "my partners and I will work harder than ever to ensure your health and welfare are looked after in the best possible way."

Appreciative cluckings.

"And now," Dr Grant says, relief in his voice that he has managed the words he had so carefully rehearsed, "please raise your glasses to the memory of Lauren. May she rest in peace."

"Lauren!"

The cry lifts to the ceiling. Tyler barks. Mouths drink.

Nausea rises from the pit of Amy's stomach and threatens to engulf her.

It was all my fault. It must've been. Mum fell off Duchess and I must've been to blame. Maybe I saw something that frightened me and Mum tried to protect me. Maybe I shouted at something and scared Duchess. Maybe Cadence started to bolt after a rabbit and Duchess threw Mum off her by mistake. Why, oh, why can't I remember?

Last night I had that dream again. I'm out on the Common and the sky is black. A strip of lightning shivers silently across it. I can

*hear the thunder of horses' hooves, but I don't know where it's coming
from. I'm terrified. I know something terrible is going to happen and
I want to scream. But when I open my mouth, I can't make a sound.
I wake and sit up in bed. I open my mouth, but nothing comes out
of it.*

Dad's arm slides across her shoulders. "Are you all right,
sweetheart?"

Amy nods.

Dad bends to whisper in her ear. "Soon they'll be gone.
These kind people who've come to pay their respects.
They'll all go home. Then you and me and Jules and Aunt
Charlotte – we can have a quiet time around the fire, just the
four of us."

Amy can smell alcohol on Dad's breath. *Just the four of us
doesn't mean with Mum any more. It can never mean that again.*

The room becomes jumpy with noise. Tyler has found a
fur hat on the pile. Amy is sure it belongs to Frances, their
vicar. She's been so kind to them since Mum died. The hat
looks damp and bedraggled. Tyler is joyfully tugging it
through the clusters of legs.

I can't even say "Bad dog!" to him.

She looks at the faces peering down at her, their pitying
watery eyes, their wagging chins. She can't bear them a
minute longer.

She ducks under Dad's arm, pushes against the bodies, crashes on all fours up the stairs into the silence of her room.

Tyler comes bounding after her.

She flings herself on her bed, face down. She remembers how she used to fling herself across Cadence to ride her, pulling at her solid, welcoming warmth, feeling the soft fall of her silvery mane.

Cadence.

She'd never ride her again. Not now. Not ever again.

Tyler jumps on to Amy's bed. He nuzzles at her ear. When there is no response, he sighs. He settles himself across Amy's back to guard her through the night.

"I'm so sorry I couldn't come yesterday," Mary says.

She kneels on the floor, beside the fire where Amy is crouching, and takes her hands. The wonderful scent of horses drifts from Mary's clothes.

"Ballard's been off her feed all week. The vet got delayed and I had to deal with it myself."

Amy wants to say, "Is Ballard going to be OK?" but the words rattle in her head instead of coming out.

"She'll be fine." Mary strokes the flop of Amy's hair away from her face. "I thought about you all day. Everybody did . . . You know that, don't you?"

Amy nods.

"Look." Mary swallows. She turns her face towards the gentle flicker of fire. "I've come with the van and I'll take Duchess away. Of course I will. And your dad's wonderful Marathon." Her voice hardens. "I know it's what Dr Grant wants."

Amy nods more vigorously. The flames dance into energetic life.

"Duchess and Marathon can join the other thoroughbreds in my fields. They'll have a marvellous life. I'll look after them for as long as you want . . . "

Rigid as a stone, Amy stares at Mary.

"For as long as your dad wants . . . "

Amy thinks, *Oh, God, I know what's coming.*

"But your beloved Cadence. Are you quite sure you want me to take her too?"

Amy freezes. Her head will no longer even nod.

"I mean, you two have grown *up* together." Mary smiles, except her eyes don't match her mouth. "Remember when I taught you to ride?"

Amy's hands, locked between Mary's, feel cold and hard as the ice she used to break on Cadence's water trough early on a winter's morning.

"You were only three." Mary's eyes begin to flicker in the firelight. "Remember?"

9

How could I forget?

"The moment I saw you on Cadence, I knew you were going to be a beautiful little rider."

I couldn't get out of Mum's car fast enough . . .

"I thought, That little Welsh pony and that Amy, they're *made* for each other."

I raced into the stable yard to find Mary, to find the new pony she'd bought for me. Mum laughed. That wonderful trill, like a bird singing. I heard her call, "Not so fast, young lady! Wait for me!"

"And now," Mary said, "you really want me to take Cadence away?"

Amy wrenches her hands out of Mary's. She stands up, steps backwards like a dancer, very carefully. One, back; two, back. She pulls out of her pocket a crumpled piece of paper. She throws it on the floor, as if it stings her skin. It flutters on to Mary's knees.

PLEASE, says the paper, TAKE CADENCE AWAY.

Mary reaches for the message. She smoothes out the crumples, but her hands are shaking. Her eyes flick, flick, pause, flick over the words. She looks up at Amy.

"I understand."

She throws the paper on the fire. It flares yellow and sooty black.

Amy spins round. She crashes out of the room, across the hall, up to the top of the stairs. She hears Dad walk out of the kitchen to the living-room door.

"Any luck?"

"None, Dr Grant." Mary's voice comes grim and sad. "Amy won't budge an inch."

"Didn't think she would."

There is a rustling.

"This is for their livery, Mary. Thank you . . . "

Dad's voice breaks.

"They're all yours now. Take them away."

Amy learned to live silently inside her own head.

She returned to her private school in Hindhead two weeks after the inquest and the funeral. She'd missed the first three weeks of the spring term and was dreading going back, but Dad said the longer she left it, the harder it would be. By the time she got there, the whole school knew what had happened. The girls in her class were great. They each gave her a hug, while the boys stood about looking uncomfortable.

The teachers were sympathetic and patient. Some of them spoke to her more loudly and more clearly than to anyone else, as if she'd suddenly gone deaf and needed to lip-read. To her great relief, none of them asked her questions in class, where her silence would have been so embarrassing she'd have died.

Her best friend, Ruth Manning, talked to her incessantly, told her not to worry, that her voice would come back, she promised. Amy nodded, wrote her a note: *I'm planning to talk non-stop for a week when it does, so stand by*. But going to Ruth's noisy, untidy, friendly house, where everyone played music all day long – Ruth's dad hammering away at their grand piano, her mum sawing at her cello, Ruth's older sister singing like a plaintive flute, Ruth herself bending and swaying to her violin – made Amy feel more silent and lonely than ever.

Dad said he wasn't a bit worried about her, he was sure everything would be "just hunky-dory, you'll see", but Amy often caught him looking at her. He started reading books called *Childhood Trauma: Its Possible Long-term Effects*, and *Memory Loss and How to Cope with It*. If Amy came into the room, he'd swiftly push them under a pile of newspapers. When he left, Amy would ferret them out and stare anxiously at the titles, biting her lip.

Julian returned to school the day after Mum's funeral. Amy wrote him long letters – she had so much *time* on her hands now she couldn't talk to Ruth – and sometimes Julian answered: quiet, careful letters, beautifully written with his fountain pen. He was teaching himself Italian; hating football; making friends with a boy called Christopher who'd just arrived at school.

He never mentioned Mum.

Amy missed her mother every day, but more sharply at certain times. Nobody bustled around the kitchen in the morning, humming bits of Mozart, making breakfast. Aunt

Charlotte never ate breakfast. Amy quickly learned to make her own. Mum wasn't there to meet her after school in her battered Mini the colour of school custard, terracotta plant pots and muddy shoes heaped in the boot. For weeks it sat in the garage and then one day it vanished. Dad said he'd given it to someone in the village, but Amy never saw it again. Aunt Charlotte's posh silver Ford with its immaculate shine made the other kids stare.

Coming back to the house after school wasn't the same with Aunt Charlotte. The fact that Amy couldn't tell her about her day made the long silences between them more painful than anything.

The stables were closed. Dad said they could sell the land, but he never got round to it. Amy avoided going anywhere near horses. The smell of hay made her vomit.

Dad gave Mum's clothes to Oxfam. Suddenly he looked ten years older. Amy saw the strain etched in new lines on his face, spotted his forced cheerfulness when he reached out his arms.

"Thank God you're still with me, darling girl," he'd whisper, but Amy often heard him crying in the night. When that happened, Aunt Charlotte would go into Dad's room.

"Don't cry, William, dear," she'd murmur. "Lauren wouldn't want it, would she?"

Everything would go quiet again and Amy would drift back into sleep.

After the first week, Amy carried a small notebook with her everywhere. She wrote brief messages in it for Dad and Aunt Charlotte:

Taking Tyler out for a walk.

Can Ruth come for supper?

Need some new trainers. Could we go to Guildford tomorrow?

She left notes for Dad on the kitchen table to try to cheer him up:

Hope you had a good day.

You're the best Dad I've ever had.

Mrs Bryant gave me top marks for my English essay.

On Valentine's Day, she propped a card decorated with an enormous heart stuffed in shiny pink satin outside Dad's door. It said, *Love you most in the whole wide world.* She pretended not to hear when Dad burst into tears and went back to his room.

At first when the phone rang, Amy raced to answer it. Then she realised she couldn't even say, "Hello." She'd mouth, "Sorry!" when Aunt Charlotte or Dad rushed to grab the phone instead, and stand feeling useless and pathetic while they asked relevant questions, scribbled notes and signalled to Amy that it wasn't in the least her fault.

Tyler didn't understand why she couldn't call to him. He'd look up at her with questions blazing from his round black eyes. She'd bend to stroke his silly, floppy spaniel ears, trying to reassure him.

Aunt Charlotte stayed on. She said she needed a break from London, but several times Amy heard her on the phone to her business partners, promising to return "as soon as possible". Once the conversation grew heated. Aunt Charlotte told the person on the other end of the line, "Don't interfere. I'll come back all in good time . . . and I'll be the best judge of when that is!"

One afternoon, during a dull half-term day when she had nothing much to do and she was missing Julian, Amy wrote a letter:

Dear Aunt Charlotte

Please don't feel you need to stay because of me. You've been great, but I'm perfectly all right now and Dad can look after me. I know your job is really important to you . . .

But she tore it up.

It seemed so ungrateful, as if she were implying she no

longer wanted her aunt to stay with them. Secretly, that was true. Amy longed to have Dad to herself, just him and her around the fire at the end of the day, in their own private world, with Tyler watching them approvingly from his basket.

And anyway, she knew why Aunt Charlotte was still with them, what she was waiting for. She wanted Amy to "get better" – to wake up one morning with a voice that could say, "Good morning", that could laugh, hum, cough, sing, scold Tyler, answer the phone, talk to Ruth. And with a memory that could give Charlotte what she most needed: an explanation – a minute-by-minute account – of her beloved sister's accident.

At the end of the spring term Amy breathed a sigh of relief. Over the Easter break, she planned to spring-clean her room, read lots of books, walk with Tyler on the Common, spend time at Ruth's, help Aunt Charlotte to cook. They were going to make a special simnel cake and decorate some chocolate eggs.

She'd learned that if she took each day as it came, she could get through it.

But on the Thursday morning before Good Friday, Aunt Charlotte rose abruptly from the table, though she hadn't drunk her tea.

"Going into Guildford to get bits and pieces," she said.

Amy saw her look quickly at Dad, then noticed him give her the smallest nod, as if they had planned something between them.

Dad ate the last of his scrambled eggs. Aunt Charlotte bustled about the hall, then the front door slammed. There was a faintly uncomfortable silence.

Dad cleared his throat.

"Before I go to the surgery, sweetheart, there's something I want to say."

Amy looked at him steadily. *He's nervous. He's trying to butter that toast, but his hand's shaking.*

"Thing is, Amy, we were wondering . . . I had a word with your headmistress and one of your teachers yesterday. They kindly met me at the surgery."

A shiver of alarm shot through Amy's heart.

"We discussed the possibility of your – of our – learning sign language. We thought it might help you . . . give you a practical way to communicate with us again."

Amy's mouth fell open.

Dad rushed on. "The teacher I met yesterday – her name's Yvonne Parker, you know, she teaches remedial classes – she can already use the system and she told me it isn't difficult.

She showed me some simple words, gave me a book about it. I'd love to learn it with you. We thought the Easter hols would be a great time to start."

Amy stared at Dad, her eyes wide and dry.

"Lots of people, if they're born deaf and can't talk —" Dad spoke rapidly now, as if he'd been practising a speech — "they use the system all the time. It's marvellous because it links them with the real world. They can do anything they want."

Amy stopped looking at Dad. She concentrated on reading the label on the jar of marmalade. Her mouth felt dry as dust.

I can just imagine what they must've said. "Thank you for making time to see us, Dr Grant. Amy's obviously no better. We're concerned about her. It's our job to watch our pupils, monitor their progress. Such a pity, Dr Grant. Amy had been doing so well. Although we still have high hopes for her future."

Dad took a deep breath. "If you don't like the idea —" his voice shook — "tell me and I'll forget about it. It's only a suggestion." He put down his knife. "I want us to face up to the fact that —"

Amy clenched her hands, forced herself to answer.

"NO," she mouthed. She pulled her notebook from her pocket and scribbled NO, NEVER on it. She tore out the note, pushed it towards him.

Dad glanced at it. He seemed to shrink a little. "OK," he said gently.

He reached across, opened Amy's fist, stroked her palm. "I understand. If I were you, I'd probably feel the same."

He came round the table to give her a hug.

Amy clung to him.

"But think about it, sweetheart. Don't dismiss it out of hand." He looked into her face. "We'll talk about it another time."

When Dad had gone to the surgery, Dora arrived. She was a neighbour who came three times a week to help with the chores. Amy waited until she heard hoovering from the bedrooms. She shut herself in the downstairs loo and burst into tears.

She knew Dad was doing his best, but the pain in his eyes this morning had cut her to the quick. As if things weren't hard enough for him without Mum. She was making everything worse. A lot worse.

She wanted to scream, make the walls rattle with noise. She couldn't even sob.

She held on to the edge of the basin. It felt cold. Her tears fell in hot splodges on to her hands. *Dad's right. I might never*

be able to speak again. Maybe Ruth could learn sign language and
we could get videophones . . .

After twenty minutes she dried her eyes, looked at her face in the mirror. A pair of grey-green eyes, red-rimmed and puffy, stared back.

She straightened her shoulders. "Pull yourself together," she mouthed.

She ran the cold tap, smoothed water on her forehead, over her shining plaits.

When she opened the door, Tyler was waiting for her, that reproachful "You haven't taken me for a walk" look in his eyes.

She mouthed at him, "You win, Tyler," and slid into her duffel coat. She scribbled a note for Dora: *Taken Tyler out on the Common*, and left it on the draining board.

Amy runs with Tyler down through the back garden and scrapes open the battered wooden gate. Then she turns left on to Ludshott Common, up the short, steep path towards the part where it gets all sandy and it's like walking along the beach. She can see for miles. The wind whips into her hair and through her clothes as if she isn't wearing anything.

Nobody's ever going to treat me as if I were permanently dumb. Because I'm not, I'm not, I'm not. I will talk again, I've promised

Dad and Aunt Charlotte and Jules and Ruth . . . I must *not let them down . . .*

She has not been back to the spot where the accident happened: a narrow, stony, badly kept path bulging with thick, snarly tree roots which snakes away from the thick wood and links the edge of the Common to her back garden. It's easily avoided, even if Tyler often starts to run there out of habit. It's as if an impenetrable wall blocks off that part of the Common, forbidding her to cross into it.

For the first time in ten grey days the sun clears through the clouds, the sky winks a newly washed blue. A breeze strokes Amy's face, shifting the fur on Tyler's back as he races ahead. Dew glitters on a thousand spiders' webs that cling to the hawthorn and the gorse, lifting and glinting.

Amy's spirit lifts with them.

When she hears the sound of horse's hooves behind her, her heart begins to thud against her ribs. It has become an immediate response to the sound haunting her recurrent nightmare.

She does not look round, but moves aside to allow the rider to pass. A brown stallion gallops by, a woman rider urging it on. Red curls dance beneath her cap.

She's got hair just like Mum's. It was so thick and curly, always escaping from any knot she tied, any hat she crammed over it.

A wave of longing to hear her mother's voice shakes her body.

Tyler races ahead. Amy turns the corner with the path and begins to jog. The words *"Mum, Mum, I want you back. Mum, Mum, I want you back"* thump in her throat.

Tyler stops to sniff another dog, a ginger Labrador called Hovis.

"Morning, Amy," Jimmy calls cheerfully. "Lovely day at last!"

Amy smiles and nods dumbly back at one of their neighbours. *It* is *a lovely day. It's spring and Easter tomorrow and Jules will be home this afternoon and I can't wait to see him.*

Then she sees Tyler's body stiffen as he spots a rabbit lolloping under an oak. He starts to bound after it. Without thinking, Amy opens her mouth.

"Tyler," she shouts. "Here, Tyler, here!"

Tyler stops dead in his tracks. He turns to look at her and then comes racing back as if blown by the wind.

Amy collapses against the nearest tree, her hands at her mouth. She says slowly, as if testing the truth of the words, "I can talk again."

Her head fills with the sound of her own voice. Blood flows to her cheeks, her legs shake with relief and joy. Tyler hurtles towards her, pawing the ground at her feet. He seems to give her strength. She picks him up and swings him in the air.

"Tyler! I can talk again! Just wait until I tell Dad and Ruth and Aunt Charlotte and Julian. They're in for such a surprise."

She puts Tyler down. He waits at her feet, looking up at her expectantly.

"*Good* dog, Tyler . . . If it wasn't for you I'd still be silent as a stone."

The relief at being able to say anything I want. I'll never take it for granted.

"Come on, Tyler. Race you home . . . "

Amy runs into the house. She rushes for the phone, grabs it with shaking hands. She's almost forgotten Ruth's number. Then it comes pattering back.

"Ruth! It's me!"

"Amy?" Ruth's voice squeals with amazement.

"Yes! Isn't it brilliant? I can talk again!"

"I can't believe it! When did you —"

"I was out on the Common with Tyler. He was behaving like an idiot as usual, chasing a rabbit!"

Tyler yaps excitedly. He pats a stray ping-pong ball across the hall.

"And there I was, yelling at him to come back!"

"God, Amy, I'm over the moon . . . I'm coming round straight away!"

"I'm going to talk for a week."

Amy puts down the phone, her hand shaking.

    She flings her arms in the air.

    She starts to sing, to dance along the hall.

    Then she freezes.

    Sure, she can talk.

    Her voice has come back.

    But not her memory.

    That morning remains a total blank . . .

Six Years Later

3

"Our last GCSE!" Amy leans her bicycle against her neat, narrow hip, shades her eyes against the afternoon sun. "I can't believe it. Do you realise we've worked years for this moment?"

"Never worked so hard in my life!" Ruth runs a hand through her dark untidy curls. She props her bike against the gutter. "It feels weird and wonderful! Ice creams to celebrate? My treat."

Amy grins. "The largest chocolate ice cream in the world and sod the calories."

"With a figure like yours, who needs to count?" Ruth vanishes inside the newsagent's. The violin she's propped in her bike basket makes the bike topple over. Amy laughs. It's typical of Ruth that even her bike has a life of its own.

She looks along the quiet village street, the familiar shops, the people – she recognises most of them – going about their business. *Nothing ever changes here. Everything's neat and tidy, in its proper place. Just the way I like it.*

She checks the coiled bun of hair at the nape of her neck. Smooth and correct. Then her bike basket. All those biology books can go back on the shelf above her desk, along with her immaculate files.

Tonight she'll cook a special supper for Dad: one of her chicken casseroles, with a summer pudding to follow. She has all the ingredients in her sparkling kitchen. She plans their meals every Saturday and shops at the Liphook supermarket with Dad in the afternoon.

This evening, they'll eat in the dining room, candles shining on the mahogany table, their serviettes in lovely silver rings. They'll walk Tyler on the Common, talk about her work for the next few months.

It's six years since Mum died. It feels longer: as if she and Dad have always lived alone together, happiest in each other's company, though delighted when Julian's home. And when Aunt Charlotte comes to stay: at Christmas and Easter, and often at weekends. Just to keep in touch, look after Amy. Make sure that Dad's OK.

Amy, almost sixteen now, is going to be a doctor. Julian's reading History of Art at Cambridge. He's always turned up his nose at medicine. "I'm much too squeamish," he'd say, shuddering at the thought of "all those bodies . . . You can be the worthy one, sis! Give me a painting any day. Bodies in paintings don't cough and bleed!"

But Amy's longing to follow in Dad's footsteps. And one

day, if she decides to be a GP, maybe she'll join his practice. He'll hand over his files. "Remember Mrs Meadows? Her son has a strange new virus . . . " Oh, yes. Her inheritance. That's what Dad's life has been about. Caring for the village folk until it's her turn to take over . . .

Ruth emerges from the newsagent's holding two huge ice creams. She hands the chocolate one to Amy, buries her face in a livid pink concoction.

Amy laughs. "You've got strawberry bits all over your nose."

"So? Part of the fun." Ruth picks up her bike with her free hand and glances at Amy. "Coming to the club in Guildford tonight? Me and Eddie are going. Pete said he'd be there."

Amy savours the coolness of the ice. "Pete who?"

"Oh, come on, Amy! Pete Franklin. You met him on Saturday, lives in Haslemere. Says he fancies you."

Amy blushes, furious with herself. "Sorry. I'm cooking for Dad."

"You can do that any night."

"No, I can't." Amy bites off a neat piece of cone. "He's usually on call. Said he'd take a night off, to celebrate the last of my exams. I'm defrosting the chicken."

Ruth swallows a dollop of ice cream. "Do you know what, Amy Grant? You're becoming more than a little dull!"

"Too bad!"

"It *is* too bad . . . Me and Eddie have been together for ages. You've never even *had* a boyfriend."

"What's the rush?" Amy says vaguely.

Ruth turns away to chat to one of her neighbours. Amy is about to join in when something catches her eye.

Somebody familiar – *very* familiar – has come out of the Indian restaurant at the end of the street.

Dad.

But he's not alone.

A tall woman with smooth dark hair cut into a short bob has come out with him. She's wearing a cream-coloured suit with a long jacket and a knee-length skirt. She's tying a scarf round her neck, talking to Dad. More than talking – they're laughing, standing close together, he's looking into her eyes.

They turn and start to cross the road. Dad flings an arm in front of her, pulls her back from an oncoming Land Rover. It looks as if they're going to the surgery . . .

"Amy?"

"What?"

"You haven't listened to a word. What are you staring at?"

"Nothing."

"Come on, tell me."

Amy swallows the last of her cone. It tastes bitter. She glances at Ruth. "I thought I saw my dad with someone."

"Who?"

"A woman. I've never seen her before. They came out of the Manzil, walked off down the road arm in arm."

"What's so extraordinary about that?"

Amy says quietly, "Dad didn't tell me he was taking anyone to lunch."

Ruth stares at her. "For goodness' sake, Amy. Does he have to tell you everything?"

"No, he doesn't *have* to . . . He just *does*."

"That's daft." Ruth takes another swipe at her unruly hair. "He's got a life of his own, hasn't he? Maybe she's one of his patients."

"She didn't *look* ill. I didn't recognise her. I'm sure she's not from round here."

Ruth pushes her bike into the road and straddles it. "There's only one way to find out. You'll have to ask him at that supper of yours tonight."

Amy stirs the rich casserole, sniffing at the pungent, honest tang of garlic which cuts like a knife through the steamy air.

"That smells wonderful!" Dad puts his head round the door. "Can I help?"

"It's all done." Amy reaches to kiss his cheek. It feels rough with a day's growth of beard. "Good day?"

"Very good." Dad smiles. His dark eyes beneath their heavy brows look brighter than usual. "Twenty out of ten."

A pang of alarm shoots through Amy's heart. "I had a good day too."

"Of course!" Dad spins round from the sink. "How was biology?"

"I could answer all the questions standing on my head."

"Great!" Dad hugs her. "I'm sure you've done brilliantly. Here, let me take the casserole."

Amy carries a bowl of new potatoes and green beans into the dining room. The scent of the roses she'd arranged on the table is drowned by the aroma of chicken.

"So," she says carefully when they've eaten. Her heart thumps uncomfortably. She forces herself to ask. "Did you find time for lunch today?"

"That was delicious, Amy. You're an excellent cook." Dad looks at the flowers. "We need to plant more roses. Keep replenishing Mum's rose garden. Maybe we could drive to the garden centre, check their new stock."

"I'd like that." Amy stands up. She stacks the summer-pudding plates. Her legs feel surprisingly weak. She says flatly, trying to seem nonchalant, aware she's doggedly repeating the question, making it into a statement, "So you didn't have lunch."

Dad folds his serviette, pushes it through the ring. He does not look up. "Guess I had a sandwich at my desk."

"He lied."

Amy sits in the hall talking to Ruth on the phone. Dad had vanished in the car on an errand and taken Tyler with him.

"An out-and-out lie. A sandwich at his desk. Why would he say that?"

"He must've had a reason."

"Yeah. He doesn't want me to know what he's doing any more."

"Nonsense. P'raps it's a question of patient confidentiality."

"Don't give me that! Not in the Manzil at lunchtime!"

"Maybe that lunch is a weekly date. We're not usually in the village so early in the afternoon. It was only because we'd taken the last exam and we had the rest of the day off. Maybe he and this woman have been to that restaurant lots of times, but you've just never seen them."

"So if she's a friend, why hasn't he told me about her?"

"Either she is someone special and he doesn't want you to know about her, or she's so unimportant he's forgotten."

Amy says slowly, "I think she's special. He said he'd had a wonderful day."

Ruth sounds impatient. "You're making a mountain out of a molehill. Why didn't you *tell* him you'd seen her and ask him who she is?"

"I can't explain." Amy curls the telephone cord round her fingers until it hurts. "I don't want to pry."

"Look, Amy. Suppose your dad *has* got a girlfriend. It's been *years* since your mum . . . "

"Six years," Amy says abruptly.

"Exactly. So why *shouldn't* he?"

"Because —" Amy is surprised and alarmed that her eyes sting with tears — "because he belongs to me."

"Hey, come on, Amy. Get a life. You're his *daughter*, not his —"

"I *know* what I am." Amy rubs the base of her right hand into her eyes. "You don't need to remind me." She hears Ruth's front-door bell ring.

"Eddie's here." Ruth's voice is flustered. "Sure you won't come with us?"

Amy stares across the hall floor. The late-evening sun filters through the stained-glass windows in the front door, dappling the tiles with rainbow-coloured, gently moving shadows.

"I'm not in the mood. Those exams have worn me out."

"You'll be sorry."

No, I won't. All that silly chat, all that noise. And Pete, with his skinny chest and big ears. Why would anyone want to spend the evening with him?

Amy goes back to the kitchen, clatters plates into the dishwasher, lays the table for breakfast. Then she runs up to the room which is her special sanctuary: Mum's study.

That day of the funeral, in the evening, when everyone had gone, she'd written Dad a note: *Please can we keep Mum's room just as it is? Not touch anything? Ask Dora to keep it clean, but not to move anything or make it different?*

Dad had nodded, immediately understood.

Now Amy opens the door. The room lies directly above her own bedroom and shares the view of the garden. Here she can see over the paved terrace leading from the house, over the lawn and the rose garden, out across the silver birch and rowan tree to the Common and the deep fir woods beyond.

The sun lies low in the June sky; a blackbird sings from the birch. Amy looks at the old sofa and slouchy chairs, the wide desk under the window, the shelves piled with books on gardening and design. Even now, when she buries her face among the cushions, she remembers the smell of Blue

Grass, the perfume her mother always wore, its pungent freshness.

One cushion in particular. Mum had made it as a present for her, that last Christmas. She'd embroidered her favourite stained-glass window from Saint Luke's: Saint Elizabeth, standing proud and stocky with her bare arms and feet, holding in her apron nine pink roses and a loaf of bread.

"*She's carrying her garden with her*," Mum always said. "*What I love about her is her strength*."

Amy raises her head.

"Something's going on, Mum. I don't know what it is and I could be wrong. But at supper tonight, Dad lied to me. That's never happened before and I'm scared."

She looks above the small stone fireplace. On the wall hangs Mum's portrait, painted by a student friend. Mum sits in a garden on a curly iron chair, behind her a pale purple lilac tree in full bloom. She wears jeans and a white shirt, the sleeves rolled to her elbows. She holds an apple, out of which she's taken a single bite. Her hair hangs loose on her shoulders, thick, curling, dark red. Amy's inheritance.

"I don't know what to do."

Mum stares down at her, the half-smile lifting her mouth, lighting her extraordinary pale grey-green eyes.

The silence in the room intensifies.

"Talk to me," Amy says. "If you were me, Mum, what would *you* do?"

4

Half an hour later Amy heard Dad's car draw up. She ran downstairs and opened the door.

Dad heaved something bulky from the boot.

She stared. "What on *earth* is that?"

"An exercise bike." Dad grinned. "They were on special offer at that new supermarket." He slammed the boot, his face red with exertion. "Hold the door open for me, Amy . . . Tyler, *please* stop snapping at my heels."

Dad staggered across the path and through the front door. He plonked the bike in the hall. Tyler skidded around it, growling.

"Where are you going to put it?"

"I thought I'd turn the garage into a gym."

"A *what?*"

"I don't get enough exercise. Couple of walks a week with Tyler doesn't count, and I've been piling on the pounds."

"*I* haven't noticed."

Dad laughed. "Your wonderful cooking doesn't help. Not that I'm complaining." He pulled affectionately at a long strand of her hair. "You look after me better than I deserve.

But as you get older, it gets harder to burn those calories."
He shifted his waistband. "These trousers feel tighter by the
minute. So I thought, William, my boy, it's action stations."

Amy looked at Dad's flushed face and untidy hair; at his
eyes, sparkling with excitement. For a moment she saw him
at sixteen, taking a girl on his first date . . . falling in love
with Mum.

She said, "The garage is a total mess. Shall I help you clear
it?"

"That'd be great. Here, let me unwrap the bike."

He tore at the wrapping. Tyler growled more loudly. The
scent of new leather and shiny chrome wafted into the hall.

"There!" Dad said, as if he'd just made it himself. "It's got
a speedometer and a clock with a timer . . . And this shows
you how many miles you've pedalled."

Amy snapped, "I have seen one before, you know."

The bike loured at them aggressively.

"Course, sweetheart, it's not just for me. I bought it for
both of us. You'll be able to use it too."

Amy lies in bed, abruptly awake. Beads of sweat on her
forehead drip into her hair. She's had the nightmare again,
the first time for ages. The thunder of horses' hooves, the
streak of silent lightning, the terror, the feeling of paralysis.

The details are always the same.

Each time the nightmare returns, she thinks, *Maybe this is the last time I'll ever have it*. But she knows she's only trying to cheer herself up.

She looks at her clock. Five in the morning.

She'll never get back to sleep now, there's no point in even trying. She throws back the sheet and blanket, slips out of bed. Her back aches. She and Dad had worked for two solid hours last night, clearing that garage.

She patters into the bathroom, reaches in the cabinet for some toothpaste. A new bottle catches her eye. She pulls it out. It's hair dye. The seal on the bottle has not been broken. *Especially for Men!* shouts the label. *Lose That Grey! Regain Your Youthful Looks!*

Amy replaces the bottle. Suddenly she feels like going back to bed. On the landing, she notices the door to Dad's bedroom stands slightly ajar. She pushes it open and peers round. Dad's pyjamas lie crumpled on the bed, his work suit swings from its hanger.

Back on the landing, she hears the kitchen door click. She shoots into her room, darts to the window, wrenches at the curtain.

Dad's running through the garden towards the Common. No, not running, he's jogging, his head slanted down, in a concentrated, purposeful way. He's wearing a bright red tracksuit with a navy stripe snaking down the sides of the legs.

Tyler races ecstatically ahead of him, his silly ears flying.

The pit of Amy's stomach heaves. She opens the window and takes a deep breath of dawn air. The first delicate swirl of birdsong rustles from the trees.

"I mean . . . " Amy pushed her bike into the school shed. "It was five in the morning, for heaven's sake. Dad *never* gets up before six-thirty if he can help it. Not unless a patient calls him out, and then he makes a terrific fuss."

"Don't you need *less* sleep as you get older?" Ruth asked.

"And that tracksuit. I've never seen it before. We buy all his clothes together, we always have done since Mum . . . "

"I think it's great." Ruth wrenched three battered library books from her bike basket. "Lots of men when they reach forty . . . How old's your dad?"

"Forty-six," Amy said sullenly.

"It's a good age to start taking yourself in hand. Most blokes go to seed – too many chips, too much beer . . . "

"I don't *give* Dad too many."

"And there's yours trying to stay fit, and all *you* can do is grumble."

43

"I'm not *grumbling*."

"You could've fooled me!"

"It's so *unlike* him. And *hair* dye! I *ask* you. I like him just the way he is."

"This lady friend." Ruth glanced at Amy as they crunched the gravelled path leading into school. "The one you saw him with."

Amy growled, "What about her?"

"Maybe he's doing all this for *her*."

Ruth pulled at the heavy glass door. The smell of school gusted out at them: disinfectant from newly washed floors, chalk and sweat.

Amy flushed. "He'd better not be!"

"Face it," Ruth persisted. "Maybe he *is*."

Amy gets home from school, wheels her bike into the garage. For a moment she thinks she's in someone else's. The bags of rubbish she and Dad had filled have gone, the brick walls and high ceiling have been cleaned of cobwebs, the concrete floor swept. Dad must've asked Dora to finish what they'd started.

Beside the new exercise bike sits a large, unopened box.

Amy tears at the wrapping. A black and yellow trampoline

stares out from a sea of white foam. *The New Rebounder: The Best Way to Fight Flab. Twenty Minutes a Day! Feel the Difference in a Week!*

Gingerly, Amy steps on it. She begins to bounce. Up! Down! Up! Down! *Higher*, she thinks angrily. *Higher!*

Her hair escapes its knot, swirls delightedly into the air.

From inside the house, Tyler barks.

For a week, Amy watched Dad more closely than ever.

The grey flecks in his hair began to tone into a new soft brown. A second tracksuit, dark green with a fierce yellow stripe, appeared in the dirty-washing basket, soaking with sweat. A new vegetable juicer sat in the kitchen.

On Saturday morning, Dad appeared with packets of rice flakes, millet flakes, raisins, sesame, linseed and sunflower seeds.

Amy looked up from her list. "Where did you get that parrot food?"

Dad said casually, "A friend of mine suggested I try something different. There's a new health-food shop in the village . . . I eat too many eggs. This makes wonderful muesli. Much better for me. For us both."

"But I've made scrambled eggs every morning for as long as I can remember."

"That's *exactly* what I mean." Dad hitched up his jeans. "I've done fifty miles on that bike this week," he said proudly.

Amy refused to congratulate him.

Dad sat at the table. "Let's go organic this week. Tons of fruit and vegetables, nuts, beans, salad. I'm going to do a strict detox."

Amy flushed. "You don't like my cooking."

"Nonsense, sweetheart. It's my new fitness regime. More exercise, healthier diet. No point in one without the other. Got to move with the times, specially if you're setting your patients a good example."

"I suppose," Amy burst out, "you want them to colour their hair."

"Wondered when you'd notice." Dad smirked. "Looks better, doesn't it?"

Amy stared at him. "I liked my old dad."

"Oh, him." Dad tilted his chair. Tyler took it as an open invitation, leapt gleefully on to his lap. "Let's say there was room for improvement."

The phone jangled from the hall.

Amy stood up. "I'll get it."

"I wonder," said the voice at the end of the line, "is that Amy?"

"Yes."

"Hi. I've heard such a lot about you."

"Oh?" Amy swallowed. "Who . . . "

"My name's Hannah. Hannah Turner." Silence. The voice hurried on. "Could I possibly speak to your dad?"

Amy glanced towards the kitchen, at Tyler scampering around Dad's feet. She turned her back on them, bent her head, murmured directly into the phone, "He's taken the dog for a walk."

"Oh." Another silence. "Then could you give him a message? Tell him lunch tomorrow will be fine."

"Lunch . . . tomorrow," Amy said, as if she were writing it down.

"Your dad was kind enough to ask me. At your house. I thought I'd have to be in Cardiff, but my plans have changed."

Amy clamped her lips together.

A third awkward silence implied that Hannah Turner was finding the conversation hard going. "I'll be at your place at one o'clock. OK?"

Amy did not answer.

"I hope *you'll* be there."

"Too right," Amy said coldly. "I'll be there." She slammed down the phone.

"Who was that, sweetheart?"

"Only Ruth. She's just broken a string on her violin."

"By the way." Amy glanced sideways at Dad as they drove to the supermarket that afternoon. The glittering sunshine had vanished beneath clouds and heavy rain. *I suppose I'd better tell him.* "Someone called Hannah Turner rang."

Dad grated the gears. "You didn't tell me."

"You'd gone out with Tyler." *Well, he was just about to.*

"Did she leave a message?"

"Something about lunch tomorrow."

Dad looked at her, then back at the road. His cheekbones had turned pink. "And?"

"Said she could come after all."

"Great!" Dad gave a puff of joy, like a pricked balloon. "We must make her something special."

"What about your new diet?"

"It can be healthy *and* special, can't it?"

"You tell me." Amy gazed between the giant firs at the drenched fields. "You might also like to tell me who Hannah Turner *is*."

"Sorry, sweetheart." Dad turned into the car park, slowed to find a space. "Haven't I mentioned her to you? I must've clean forgotten."

Amy said savagely, "I wonder why. She obviously knows about me."

"Hannah Turner," Dad said, as if there were something magic about the name he was rolling round his tongue. He slid into a parking slot. "Hannah Turner's our new doctor. Brian Cooper retired last month. He should have gone at Christmas, except we couldn't spare him."

Raindrops bounced triumphantly on the windscreen.

"Hannah's our replacement. We're *terribly* lucky to have her. She's highly qualified – spent the last three years in Kenya – and we wanted a woman doctor because lots of our patients feel more comfortable with – I mean, they've been asking for a woman. She's the right age and everything."

Amy opened her mouth. "How old *is* she?"

"Thirty-one," Dad said, a wistful lilt in his voice. "She's only thirty-one."

Amy stared at him angrily. "When does she start?"

Dad turned to her.

"Hannah started last Monday. She's been with us for a week . . . "

He smiled.

"It's *flown* by."

5

Amy sits on Ruth's bed and the untidy squash of duvet while Ruth struggles into tight black jeans. Downstairs, she can hear Ruth's sister singing in a wobbly soprano: "Oh, for the wings, for the wings, of a dove . . . "

"I could do with a pair of those." Amy looks crossly at a fingernail where her newly applied Flirty Pink varnish has smudged.

"A pair of what?" Ruth's voice is muffled in a silver top.

"Wings."

Ruth's head emerges. "What do you want wings for?"

"To fly away."

"Just because your dad has asked Hannah Turner to lunch? Isn't that a bit drastic?"

"He's been interviewing for a new doctor for months, yet when he finds her, he doesn't even bother to *tell* me."

"Why *should* he?" Ruth sits at her dressing table, which is so cluttered there isn't space for her elbows. "It's not as if you have a say in it."

"Because we have a special relationship." Amy smears more varnish on the offending nail, but her hand shakes. "We always have had, ever since Mum . . . "

"Sure." Ruth looks at her through the mirror. "You were nine when it happened. It was terrible and you've coped brilliantly. But next month you'll be sixteen." She picks up a brush she's spotted among the bottles and begins to deal with her hair. "There's all the difference in the world."

"No, there isn't." Amy flushes. "I feel just the same about Dad." She looks at Ruth in the mirror. "If anything, I love him even more."

"Maybe you shouldn't."

"How can you *say* that? You don't have a *choice* of how much you love the people in your life."

"What I mean is —" Ruth tugs at her curls — "you should be concentrating on other people . . . "

"You mean boys."

"Exactly. Guys your own age."

Amy glares at her. "They're boring."

"You don't give them a chance."

Amy knows this is true. She also knows there *is* someone else in her life, but she's not telling Ruth. Not yet, anyway. She slithers off the bed, attempts to straighten the duvet, which has never been straight in its life.

She pulls her jacket over her shoulders. "Come on, then. Time to get bored out of my brain."

Ruth extracts her scarlet cardigan from underneath a pile

on the floor. "This new doctor, is she the woman you saw outside the Manzil?"

"Probably," Amy says glumly. "I haven't told Dad I saw them together. Haven't even asked him what she looks like. After tomorrow I shan't need to. All I know is she's fifteen years younger than he is and he'll see her every day."

"Give her a chance. You might even *like* her."

"I guess Dad already likes her enough for both of us."

"You don't *know* that, Amy. P'raps he's asked her to lunch because it's a nice way to welcome his new doctor."

"It's more than that. When I saw them outside the Manzil, they looked *right* together."

Ruth shrugs. "What are you going to give her for lunch?"

"Pigswill on burnt toast?"

"Delicious. I hope you'll make enough for second helpings."

Dad glances across the kitchen at Amy. His face, flushed from cooking, has a smile about it, as if he's heard a funny but secret joke.

"We're nearly there. Watercress soup in the fridge. Fresh raspberries with meringue on the sideboard. Scottish salmon and new potatoes cooked and cooling. Salads dressed and only the mayonnaise to make. How's that for a morning's work?"

Amy says sourly, "I hope she'll appreciate it."

"I'm *sure* she will." Dad begins to separate some eggs. "Could you lay the table?"

Amy hesitates in the doorway. "Where should I put her?"

Dad looks up. "What d'you mean?"

"I mean," Amy says deliberately, "should I lay a place for Dr Hannah Turner in Mum's chair?"

Dad pauses for a fraction of a second. "Might as well," he says.

When the doorbell rings, he rushes to answer it, scuttling down the hall like an excited crab. Amy ducks into the living room, stands by the window listening to the murmur of voices.

Dad says, more loudly, "Come and meet my daughter."

Amy turns.

Dad stands in the doorway, holding a spray of pink carnations, looking excited and shy. He seems suddenly lost for words.

Beside him, smiling, a woman with smooth, dark hair says, "Hi, Amy. I'm delighted to meet you. I gather you've finished your exams. Well done!"

Amy moves towards her, holds out a reluctant hand.

Hannah's feels cool and smooth. "Hello." She takes a deep breath. The seductive scent of lily-of-the-valley rises from Hannah's bare arms. "I've seen you before."

"Really?" Dad looks taken aback.

"Last week. At lunchtime. I saw you with Dad, coming out of the Manzil."

Dad touches Hannah's shoulder. "That was the day you finally agreed to join us, after all my months of persuasion." He looks at Amy. "Hannah's had to move from Cardiff. She's been incredibly efficient about it . . . I didn't want her to go home dying of hunger."

Amy curls her lips. "I *see*."

"Anyway," Dad says defensively, "you never mentioned it."

Amy goes on looking at Hannah. She has dark-lashed, hazel-coloured eyes and a perfect complexion. "Of course not. I'm always the soul of discretion. You often take ladies out to lunch, don't you, Dad?"

Dad gives a dismissive snort. "Don't be ridic—"

"I never like to pry into his private life," Amy cuts in. She winks at Hannah in a conspiratorial fashion. "But the stories I could tell . . . "

Hannah doesn't look in the least put out. She smiles teasingly at Dad. "Dr William Grant, you *are* a dark horse! Tell me your dreadful secrets."

Dad flushes. He avoids Amy's eyes, thrusts his nose into the carnations. "These are perfect. I must put them in water . . . Shall we have a drink on the terrace?"

"Good idea," Amy says. "I expect we could *all* do with a drink . . . I'll have a very large gin."

"I don't think so!" Dad throws an arm round Hannah's shoulder. She tips her head back so it almost touches his. This time they both laugh.

Oh, my God. She's beautiful.

"Your garden's *fantastic*."

Hannah stood on the terrace, looking out at the lawn and the rose garden. Tyler had scampered in an interested fashion around her legs. After she'd made a fuss of his ears, he settled panting by a chair to watch. "It must be lots of work."

"It's entirely Mum's design," Amy said quickly. "It looks incredibly beautiful this time of year . . . Dad and I don't have time to look after it, but we still have the gardener Mum used . . . great friend of ours . . . Joe Thomson, lives round the corner. Very upset when Mum died."

She looked sideways at Dad.

He'd cupped one of his hands round Hannah's elbow and was pouring white wine into her glass.

"Mum was brilliant," Amy chattered relentlessly. "At art college she came top of her year. She wrote two books on landscape design. The first won an award and her publishers sold it to the Gardening Club as a Christmas special. We still get money from it, all these years later."

"Really?" Hannah said.

Amy warmed to her theme. "Mum'd walk into a scruffy dump of weeds and old fencing, and within minutes she'd work out how it could be transformed."

"Fascinating." Hannah took a long swallow of wine.

"Everyone in the village knew her, didn't they, Dad?"

"I suppose they did," Dad said reluctantly.

"We only had to walk down the road and someone would ask her advice . . . These days there are lots of gardening programmes on TV. I'm sure if Mum were alive, she'd be doing one. They asked her to speak on *Gardeners' Question Time*, but —"

"Cheers," Dad interrupted firmly.

He'd raised his glass to Hannah, she'd clinked hers with his. She was smiling into his eyes. Her long silver earrings swung gently beneath her hair.

"Sit in the shade," Dad said. "It's going to be hot this afternoon."

Hannah slid gracefully into a deckchair. Her short denim

skirt rode up her bare thighs, her toenails glittered tangerine in the sun. "After Kenya, nothing will ever be hot."

"Africa! I find it hard to imagine you there."

"Then I'll have to tell you all about it," Hannah said, but so quietly she obviously did not intend Amy to hear.

Amy stared at them. "Could I have some orange juice?" she said loudly.

Dad had pulled his chair closer to Hannah's. He tilted his face towards Amy. "Sorry, sweetheart, I forgot. There's some in the fridge. While you're in the kitchen, could you take out the watercress soup and put it on the table?"

He took a long sip of wine, staring with admiration at Hannah's glinting thighs.

Amy turned, retreated to the kitchen.

She flung open the fridge, pulled out the soup. Shreds of watercress floated on its top like handfuls of drowning confetti.

I know what I'd like to do with this. Chuck it over them both.

"Yes," Ruth said, "but did you *like* her?"

Amy swiped viciously at a gorse hedge with Tyler's special stick. They were on the Common with him late that Sunday afternoon.

"Ask a daft question. I've no intention of liking Hannah Turner."

"God, Amy, give the woman a chance."

"Why *should* I?"

"Because she deserves one. Imagine how you'd feel if you'd met someone you wanted your dad to like."

"That isn't going to happen."

"Of course it is. Any day now, you might –"

"And anyway, it'll be different."

"Why?"

"Because of Mum."

"So what are you saying? That your mum prevents your dad from liking anyone else ever again? From having new friends? Maybe from having a new lover?"

Amy flinched at the word. She threw the stick for Tyler. Yapping with joy, he raced after it. "Mum and Dad had a perfect marriage."

"How do you know?"

Amy stared at Ruth. "I do, that's all. Dad adored her. They met when they were still at school. I never heard them quarrel. They liked the same things. They loved Jules and me. They –"

"What you mean is, you've never questioned anything. I'm not saying your dad *wanted* the accident to happen . . . "

"So what *are* you saying?"

"That maybe you put your mum on a bit of a pedestal."

"No, I don't."

"You can't help it. You remember the good bits about her and forget the bad."

Amy looked across the Common at the sun, low in the sky, threading the clouds with skeins of deepest gold. "The only thing I've 'forgotten'," she said slowly, "is the accident. I'd give *anything* to remember it."

"I'm sorry." Ruth's voice softened. She slipped an arm across Amy's shoulders and the two girls hugged each other. "I didn't mean to bring that up."

"I know." Amy stepped away and looked at her. "You're the best friend I could ever have. I only grumble with you because I can tell you anything and I know you'll listen."

She turned to look at the path where she and Mum had been riding that morning. "I still can't go back there, you know."

"Are you sure?" Ruth's eyes searched Amy's face. "Maybe if you could retrace your steps . . . even get on a pony again? Cadence is still at Mary's stables . . . "

Amy shuddered. "I feel sick at the thought." She wiped a hand over her forehead. "I'm terrified that if I go back there, I'll lose my voice again — and this time it'll be for good."

Ruth took her hand. "That'll never happen."

"I couldn't go through it again." Amy's voice shook. "It was the most humiliating thing . . . But Ruth, it's worse than that."

"How d'you mean?"

"It's six years since the accident. I've blanked it hard and fast. And when I ask myself *why* . . . " Amy looked at Ruth.

"Yes?"

"It's because something terrible must've happened."

"We *know* it did. Your mum was killed."

"But I don't think it *was* 'an accident'."

"What?"

"Mum didn't fall off Duchess just like that. She was an experienced rider. She knew the Common like the back of her hand. We'd ridden that path together hundreds of times. We weren't even riding fast. It was snowing. We'd have been extra careful."

"What are you saying?"

"That somebody else was involved."

Ruth gasped. "That it was deliberate?"

"I don't know. The police never found the tracks of any other horse because of the snow . . . They couldn't even *begin* to investigate. It took them hours to find Duchess and Cadence. They'd wandered off on to the Common. They were lost and confused, just like me." She swallowed. "There was an inquest, but it was only a formality."

Ruth stood stock-still. "But why should anyone *want* to kill your mum? She was a lovely person."

"Yes," Amy said quietly. "She was."

"So what on earth could she have done to deserve that?"

Amy screwed up her eyes, trying not to cry. The trees on the Common swayed around her. Tiny flies buzzed against her hair. She looked at Ruth's face, pale beneath its tan.

"Do you think I haven't asked myself that question, every single day, for six years?"

6

"So . . ." Dad said the following evening. "What did you think of Hannah?"

Amy stared straight ahead. "All right, I suppose."

Dad bit his lip. "Only all right?"

Amy shot him a glance. "What d'you *want* me to say?"

Dad flushed. "That you *liked* her. She certainly likes you."

"No, she doesn't. I could be anybody. She's just trying to cosy up to you."

"That's a very cynical thing to say."

"As far as Hannah Turner is concerned –" Amy's voice was full of sulk – "I'm merely your daughter, part of the package whether she likes it or not."

Dad flung back his chair. "That's not fair. If you must know, I thought you gave her a very hard time. You talked *endlessly* about Mum. It got quite embarrassing."

"So now you're embarrassed to discuss your own wife!"

Dad said coldly, "You know exactly what I mean."

"What you *mean* is that Hannah Turner's going to eclipse everything."

Dad looked her squarely in the eyes. "For a girl who's

almost sixteen, you can sometimes talk the most ridiculous childish rubbish I've ever heard." He stood up. "I'm taking Tyler for a walk. And if you *don't* mind, I'd rather go alone."

Amy shrugged. "Suit yourself. See if I care."

At the beginning of July, Dad announced he wanted to have the house decorated.

"If we start it now," he said over breakfast, "it'll be ready for the end of term and Julian coming home and your birthday party. I want the house to look fabulous. By the way —" his voice warmed — "Hannah says she'd love to help with the party. In any way she can."

Amy found it impossible to swallow another mouthful of Dad's concocted muesli. "This stuff is tasteless."

"Cut an apple into it," Dad said cheerfully. "Or a banana."

He pushed a bowl of fruit in Amy's direction. Amy ignored it.

Dad persevered. "So, what do you think?"

He's doing this for Hannah, just to show off, to impress her. He'd never bother if it weren't for her.

"I like the house as it is."

"It's grubby and frumpy. I haven't bothered with it for years."

"Dora does a brilliant job."

"Dora's wonderful at keeping it clean, but it needs more than that. Everything needs a lick of paint. The walls, the woodwork. The downstairs rooms need new wallpaper. Then we can choose some good-quality carpet, run it right through the house. Tyler's scrabbled at so many corners and the stairs are threadbare."

Amy stood up, dumped her bowl in the sink. There was something childlike and endearing about Dad's enthusiasm. She relented.

"Can I help choose the wallpaper and the paint?"

"Of *course*, sweetheart." Dad sounded relieved. "I'll bring some samples home tonight. We can look at them together."

That afternoon, after school, Amy and Ruth take the bus to Guildford. Ruth has to go to a concert her parents are giving that weekend. She needs what her mother calls a "posh frock".

It takes them two hours of fierce shopping in the crowds to find an outfit Ruth likes: a long blue chiffon skirt with an off-one-shoulder top. By the time Amy gets home it's half-past six. She's hot, tired and dusty. The heatwave louring from grey skies is oppressive.

The house looks as if an army has plundered it. Paint-spattered dust sheets cover the hall. The furniture in the living room is piled into the centre. Three of its walls are stripped, revealing rough, bare patches. Cans of unopened paint, rolls of sandpaper and bundles of brushes cluster in corners, along with an old radio and empty lunchboxes. The tang of paint-stripper drills into the air.

Amy looks at the stairs. Dust sheets flow over them like a waterfall. Dread grips her heart. *They've been in Mum's room. I'd no idea the work would start so soon . . .*

She races up the stairs to the landing, then up the second flight. The dust sheets, sliding beneath her feet, reach into Mum's study. Amy pauses in the doorway, afraid to look. The furniture is piled into an ugly central huddle. Mum's portrait is missing; the grate yawns, empty of flowers. A filthy tartan rug sprawls across the hearth. The window gapes, as if someone thought the room needed a good airing.

A knot of anger clenches Amy's stomach. *This is a special place. Now strangers have poked about in it, as if it belonged to them. How dare they?*

She slides across the floor to the window. The paint on the ledge has been scraped away; scrolls of it lie like snail shells along the skirting board. She glances down at them, bends to pick one up, feels it crack.

And then she notices.

Wedged between the dust sheet and the skirting board, against the wall where Mum's desk had stood, is a postcard. Faded, bent, lucky to have survived.

Only half curious, without thinking, Amy picks it up.

On the front, thick with dust, is a photo of Michelangelo's *David*. The head is beautiful, the limbs ripple with energy, the voluptuous mouth pouts, firm and silent, the eyes stare into space.

A black foreboding throbs in Amy's throat. *I should throw this away. Tear it up, fling it out of the window, watch it flutter into the sky.*

Instead, she turns the card. She looks at the message.

The pale-blue handwriting, delicate, flowing, stretches the width of the card. There is no date, no stamp and no address, so it must have been posted in an envelope.

I'm prying. I'm dipping without permission into Mum's private world.

But she cannot resist. One by one, the words sear into her eyes:

Lauren, my darling

I cannot believe you have left. Florence is now for me like an empty tomb. I am lost without you. It has been the happiest three

*days of my whole life. When can I see you again? Any time, any-
where. Just tell me and I'll be there.*

I am ever your own
Marcello

Amy feels colour flood her face.

She reads the words over and again, turning the card in
her hand as if she is cooking it over a spit. Frantically, she
scrabbles at the edges of the skirting board in case they
conceal another trophy.

They do not.

She stands at the window, trembling.

Florence.

Mum went to Florence the summer before she died. Amy
frowns, desperately trying to remember. Mum had taken
Julian with her, to look at paintings. Dad had been too busy
to leave the practice. He and Mum had thought Amy was too
young to go trailing around art galleries.

Mum had needed to see a landscape designer she'd met in
London, to check the details of his Italian house and garden
that featured in a book she'd been writing.

One she'd never finished . . .

Their trip had been the beginning of Julian's passion for
paintings and the Italian language.

But that's as much as Amy can remember. She cannot recall ever having talked to Mum or Julian about their trip. Nothing had seemed any different when they'd returned. They hadn't brought back any photos – or none that she remembered.

So who is this Marcello and what happened in Florence? When had he written to Mum? Had they met again, after that summer? In England? In London? Even, perhaps, in Grayshott? Did Dad know of Marcello's existence?

Dad . . .

From far away in the house, the front door slams.

Amy jumps.

"Amy?" Dad calls. "Are you up there, sweetheart?"

Amy skids over the dust sheets to the door. "I'm coming down."

"I've got some colour charts. Isn't this terrific? The decorators have made a great start!"

Amy races over the dust sheets, slithers down the stairs. She darts into her room, stares at it wildly, shoves the card under her pillow, smoothes the bed neat and tidy. She turns to leave the room, catches sight of her reflection. Her eyes stare out at her, green-black with shock.

In the kitchen she says coldly, "Why d'you have to muck about with Mum's study?"

Dad glances at her from a pile of letters. "We're doing up the whole house, Amy. I told the decorators: begin at the top and work down. And start on the living room."

"You could have left Mum's room alone."

"Look, sweetheart." Dad flings a weary arm over Amy's shoulder. "They're giving the room a simple coat of paint." He stabs at the chart. "How about this duck-egg blue? Then they'll put everything back exactly as before. You won't notice the difference."

Amy pulls away from him.

I already notice the difference. I've found a postcard and everything has changed.

Amy had been counting the days until Julian returned from Cambridge.

He'd rung the night before. "I'm on my way, sis, first thing tomorrow." She doodled through morning classes, ducked out of afternoon tennis and cycled home.

He was sitting on the terrace, under the shade of the birch. Amy saw him before he saw her. "Jules!"

He leapt to his feet. "Hi, sis! How are you?" He whirled her in his arms. "Nearly sixteen! I can't believe it."

Amy returned his hug. "I'm so glad you're home."

"Me too." Julian grinned at her. "You look great!"

Amy blushed. "Thanks."

"So does the house! What a difference!"

"Yeah," Amy said reluctantly. "It looks OK."

"You don't sound very enthusiastic."

"You know why Dad's done it, don't you?"

"It was grotty, that's why. Nothing had been touched since Mum . . . "

"It's nothing to *do* with Mum." Amy dumped her school bag on the terrace table. "It's because there's a new woman in his life."

Julian laughed. "You're kidding." He followed Amy into the kitchen.

"I wish I was." Amy took a jug of lemonade from the fridge and poured some into two glasses. She handed one to Julian. "Her name's Hannah Turner."

"But she's the new doctor."

Amy flushed. She gulped at the cool liquid. "How did you know?"

"Dad wrote to me. Said he'd found somebody brilliant to take over from Brian Cooper. You don't mean he's *seeing* her?"

"*Exactly*. I bet that's why she got the job. He fancied her."

"Good for Dad!"

"He's trying to lose weight, he's become a total health

freak, he goes jogging at the crack of dawn, he's turned the garage into a gym . . . He's even dyeing his hair."

"I'm impressed!" Julian said wryly. "All that for a woman . . . Have you met her?"

"She came one Sunday," Amy said sulkily. "For lunch."

"Wow!" Julian ran his fingers through his hair. Amy noticed it was longer, lay smooth and flat almost to his shoulders. "So what's she like?"

Amy met his eyes. "Young." She swallowed. "Fifteen years younger than Dad. And beautiful."

"Oh, *well*," Julian said teasingly. "I can't *wait* to meet her!"

"This isn't a *joke*, Jules . . . "

"Lighten up, sis. Isn't it about time Dad had some fun in his life?"

Amy said stiffly, "He has plenty of fun. He loves his job, he loves Grayshott, he loves you and me . . . "

Julian looked at her. "Yes, sis." There was a note of patience in his voice which made Amy feel patronised. "But maybe he needs to love someone who isn't a patient, a neighbour – or one of his own kids!"

"I don't think he *should*." Amy's voice sounded shrill, as if she were talking to a crowded room, not merely her brother in his jeans and crisp white shirt. "I think he should honour Mum's memory."

Julian stroked her shoulder. "He's *done* that. For six years."
His voice was gentle now, sympathetic. "That's one hell of a
long time, sis. He's only human, isn't he?"

Amy waited for two days before she summoned the courage
to show Julian the card. She'd kept it in her desk, peeped at
it, slid it guiltily back into its hiding place. *Perhaps I should
pretend I never found it. Tear it up. Burn it. Forget about it.* A
proverb echoed in her mind: *Let sleeping dogs lie.*

But something crucially important stood between Amy
and the card. Her loss of memory; knowing that her
mother's death was still, all these years later, shrouded in
mystery. Suppose the card held a vital clue to what had
happened that January morning?

She'd tell only Julian. Not Ruth. To tell Ruth would feel
cheap and nasty, like betraying Mum to an outsider. And she
certainly couldn't tell Dad. Fat chance of getting the truth
out of him, even if he knew it. Just Jules.

Because he'd remember that summer in Florence,
wouldn't he? Dad hadn't even been there. So it was up to
Jules to tell her the truth. Even if it did mean digging up the
past, with all its pain.

She read the card for the umpteenth time . . .

*

72

After supper that evening, Dad received an urgent call from an elderly patient. He rushed out to see her. Amy grabbed Julian's hand, pulled him into the garden.

"Come on," she said firmly. "We're taking Tyler out on the Common. I need to talk to you. Somewhere private, where we won't be overheard."

"What's the big secret?" Julian opened the garden gate for her. "Is it about Hannah? Dad does seem besotted."

"For a change," Amy said bitterly, "this is nothing to do with Hannah Turner." She slid her hands into her skirt pocket to make sure the card was safe. "It's to do with someone Mum knew. Someone I never met."

Julian shot her a startled glance. "What the hell are you on about?"

There'll be no going back once I've asked him. Get on with it.

She took a deep breath. "Does the name Marcello mean anything to you?"

Julian stopped dead in his tracks. In the quiet woods only the blackbird sang.

He forced a grin. "Is he your new boyfriend?"

"Don't be daft, Jules . . . Marcello's not an English name."

"I suppose not." He looked away.

Amy said quickly, "So, come on, tell me. *Do* you remember him?"

"I'm afraid I do."

Prickles of alarm dusted Amy's limbs. "Why afraid?"

"Marcello," Julian said reluctantly, as if the name stuck in his gullet, "was the guy Mum and I flew to Italy to see."

"In Florence?"

"The summer before she died."

Amy persevered. "So you met him in Florence?"

"Yes. And at . . . " He bit his lip and was silent.

"What was he like?"

Julian shook his head, as if to brush the memory aside. "Why bring him up now? It's all a hell of a long time ago."

"You're not answering my question. What can you tell me about him?"

He looked at her strangely. "How do you know his name?"

"I found something in Mum's study. The day the decorators started. They'd moved all the furniture . . . "

"So you were poking about in her things?"

Amy flushed with indignation. "Course not! I happened to spot it on the floor."

Julian frowned. "This all sounds a bit ominous."

"Does it?" Anger began to pump through Amy's veins. Instead of answering her questions, Jules was playing for time.

"*What* did you find?" There was irritation in his eyes now, and an impatience that frightened her.

She pulled the card out of her pocket. "This." She thrust it into Julian's hands, heard the quick intake of his breath.

She watched him read the message, turn the card and look at the photograph, then scan the words again. His hand shook.

"Well?" Her voice was sharp. "What do you think of that?"

Julian looked at her, his dark eyelashes flickering. "Tear it up, sis. You don't want to know."

"Of *course* I do. Why else would I have kept it?"

Julian said deliberately, "This card was sent to Mum. It's private. It's all in the past. Don't start digging around."

"But I must," Amy said wildly.

"You've no idea what you'll find."

"Don't you understand?" She snatched at the card, rammed it into her pocket. "I owe it to Mum – to her memory – to find out what was going on."

"You owe her nothing. You've paid the price of her death a thousand times."

"And you're the only person who can tell me."

Julian's face was pale. "Oh, no. Don't put this on me. I'm not getting involved." His voice was low. "And I warn you. I *beg* you. Don't take this any further. Please, sis. Don't play with fire."

For a moment he looked at her, a closed expression veiling his eyes. Then he turned abruptly and walked away, Tyler at his heels.

"Jules! Where are you going?"

"Home, where I belong!"

"But I need to *talk* to you."

He flung over his shoulder, "You know what playing with fire means, don't you?"

Amy's eyes stung with tears.

"You'll get burnt."

Amy does not follow her brother. She watches him walk away, while a sense of creeping desolation falls around her like the beginnings of dusk.

Julian has always been on her side. She can talk to him, assumes he'll listen, sympathise, tug her plaits, tease her seriousness and coax her into laughter. Now he knows more than he'll tell her, something about Mum she desperately needs to know.

Now she's on her own.

She turns back to the Common, wanders disconsolately towards a wooden bench. For a long miserable hour she sits hunched over her knees. Birds pipe their last few songs. The sun dips and dies into its crimson-pillowed bed.

I have a choice. I can either tear up the card and pretend I never found it. Or I can treat it as the first clue. I can follow its thread, discover where it leads.

"Lauren, my darling . . ."

What was it Ruth had said? *"You put your mum on a bit of a pedestal."*

What if Ruth is right?

Amy stands up, shivering. Her bare arms prick with damp; the woods have settled into twilight shadows. She looks towards the path where Mum died. In her head she hears again that thunder of horses' hooves.

I was wrong. I haven't got a choice. I don't know who Marcello is, but I'm going to find out. Whatever it takes, I'm going to discover the truth behind his words.

Nobody else cares any longer.

Only me.

7

Breakfast next morning was unusually silent.

Dad spotted it immediately. He came to the table, glowing after his run and his shower. Amy wrinkled her nose. The heavy scent of pine wafted around the kitchen.

"What's the matter with you two?"

Julian poured himself a cup of coffee.

"Well?" Dad glanced at Amy. "End of term today, your party on Saturday, your club expedition to Paris coming up. You should be dancing on air, not sitting there with a face like a wet weekend." He picked up his bag. "Wish I had six weeks off!"

"Got a headache," Amy said sullenly, but Dad had vanished through the door.

Julian said, "No, you haven't."

"It's my head, not yours."

"Come on, sis. You've got the grumps." Pause. "What have you decided to do?"

"About the card?"

He scowled. "What else?"

Amy didn't miss a beat. "Took your advice." Once the lie

had flown out, it was easy to embellish. "I tore it into shreds and chucked it away."

Julian beamed. "What a relief! I worried half the night."

"Not much else I *can* do." She stood up to clear the table. The card, wedged into her pocket, seemed to burn its way into her thigh, as if indignant at the threat of destruction. She remembered Hannah's thighs, gleaming in the sun.

Julian stood up too. "Forget about it." Gently, he punched her shoulder. "It's easy to get trapped in the past. That won't happen to you, will it, sis? You will move on."

"You mean like Dad?" Amy said bitterly.

Julian chuckled. "That's exactly what I mean." He ruffled her hair. *I wish Jules wouldn't do that. He still treats me like a child.*

"By the way, I forgot to tell you." Julian watched her approvingly. "Christopher rang."

Amy's heart missed a beat. "How is he?"

"Fine. We're going to Perugia together."

Amy concentrated on rinsing the dishes. "Oh?"

"I met a guy there last year, while I was on their summer university course. Said he'd give me a couple of weeks' intensive tuition, so I can brush up my Italian."

"Does it need brushing?"

"I can *read* it well, for my art history, but I never get a chance to speak it . . . Chris said he'd come with me. We'll probably go on to Rome or Naples."

Amy's mouth tasted sour with jealousy. "Lucky you." *A week in Paris tramping round the Louvre, with Mrs Baxter organising every moment, is hardly competition.*

"Chris is coming here to stay for a few days. I told him about your party."

Amy's heart made up for lost time. "You did?"

"He says he'd love to come. If that's OK with you."

Amy blazed a smile at her adorable brother. "It'll be *great* to see him again."

"He'll be here on Friday. He's always had a soft spot for you. Often asks me how my lovely little sister's getting on."

Amy turned away to hide her scarlet cheeks.

Move on . . . That's so easy to say.

Amy cycled over to collect Ruth for the last morning of term.

Ignore problems, shove them under the carpet, don't confront anything that looks remotely difficult. Typical of Jules. He can't bear to look at a real body, only an imitation that's been painted and clamped into a frame. That can't talk back, tell you things you'd rather not hear.

There must've been something serious going on between Mum

and Marcello to make Jules refuse to talk about it.

Mum had never finished her book with its section on Marcello's garden. But supposing somebody else had written about it? If she caught the bus to Guildford this afternoon, she could go to the bookshop. Begin to track *something* down.

Anyway, she had nothing even half decent to wear for the party. And if Chris was coming, a new outfit was essential. In fact, Chris's imminent arrival put Amy's sixteenth birthday in a whole new light.

She bumped over Ruth's driveway, trilling her bell to announce her arrival.

The three days to Friday began to shimmer with anticipation.

Amy stared out of the bus window on her way to Guildford as the small towns bumbled past – Haslemere, Godalming, Farncoombe – green and sleepy in the hazy afternoon light.

Christopher.

She'd met him twice before. Each meeting seared indelibly into her mind. The first time she'd been thirteen. Dad had taken her to Oxford, to an open day at Julian's boarding school during the summer term.

In the afternoon there'd been a cricket match. Amy stood on the sidelines, mesmerised by one of the batsmen. He made sixty powerful, energetic runs, swinging the ball to the boundary, before he was deftly caught.

A shower of hands clapped as he left the field.

Julian called out, "Well played!", grabbed his arm as he came striding from the pitch. "Chris, this is my dad – and my sister, Amy."

She caught her breath as Chris took off his helmet, looked down at her and gripped her hand. He seemed filled with sunlight, his narrow face tanned, his shirt damp with sweat, open at the neck, his dark-blond hair glistening.

He smiled at her. "Hi, Amy." His voice was deep and husky. "I've heard such a lot about you from Jules."

Dad said, "Shall we have some tea?"

"Good idea." The world became two blue eyes. "I'll jump in the shower."

The second time had been a year ago, at Cambridge, where Chris had played the title role in *Hamlet* at an Arts Theatre student production. He was reading English at Peterhouse, desperate to become an actor, but his parents insisted he got a degree first.

She and Dad had met Julian and Chris by the river. They'd gone punting, Chris standing tall and slim at the helm – "Let me do all the hard work, why don't you!" – the pole, smooth and shiny with water, dripping through his hands, his eyes flirting with her when the others weren't looking.

That evening Amy sat through *Hamlet*, her heart thumping like a drum, trying not to let Dad and Julian see how smitten she was. Neither of them ever suspected her feelings, how she'd replayed that weekend, that special evening, in her head, over and again. She'd never even told Ruth.

Dad's not the only one who's madly in love! What if he knew? That'd give him something to think about besides his darling Hannah!

And now on Friday she and Chris would meet again. She wondered what he'd make of Grayshott and Terra Firma. She wondered what he'd make of *her*. Because she didn't feel like "Julian's little sister" any more.

Nor, she realised with a jolt, did she any longer feel like "Daddy's little girl".

So what exactly *was* she?

Standing on the second floor of Guildford's Waterstone's, Amy gazed through the window at the High Street. She'd spent an hour thumbing through books on gardening and landscape design, full of marvellous photographs, elegant, beautiful – and useless.

None of them even mentioned Italy.

I don't know what I expected to find. All I have is a first name and the link with Florence. It's not much to go on. If I were serious about all this, I'd fly to Italy and find Marcello himself!

She gave a sudden laugh at the idea. A book-browser looked up at her curiously. Amy headed for the stairs. Sure, she needed to know who Marcello was. But she'd never been abroad on her own. Dad would never let her go. And she could hardly tell him the reason for the trip.

Anyway, she wasn't *that* interested.

Or was she?

Thoughtfully, she sat over a cappuccino in Starbucks, spooning up the frothy chocolate topping. Mum had left her some money in her will, in a trust fund until Amy was sixteen. She knew that Dad's chief birthday present would be her own bank account and cashcard.

Suppose she took out enough money to pay for a trip to Florence? Could she get there and back without Dad knowing? Instead of going to Paris with Mrs Boring Baxter, suppose she used that week to go to Italy?

Would she have the courage to do it on her own?

Maybe. It needed careful planning. She'd start thinking on the bus. Meanwhile, the party. Amy drained her cup. She wanted a dress, or a long skirt and frilly top: something floaty and romantic. To make Christopher sit up and say, "Hey! Just look at Jules's little sister now!"

I'm gonna take midsummer night and make it special just for you . . .

The latest pop lyric blared through the shopping arcade. Amy began to hum along.

"I've got a surprise for you," Dad said that evening.

"Oh?" Amy sliced some tomatoes. She did not bother to look up.

"For your party. Actually, it was Hannah's idea."

I might have guessed.

"She and I had lunch together. In the garden. She was saying how beautiful it looked. *Then* she said, 'Why don't we get an electrician to put some fairy lights in the trees?' It's a *brilliant* idea. They'll look fantastic."

Amy's heart lurched. She imagined standing in Christopher's arms in the rose garden, the moon shining, the lights sparkling from the silver birch, music from the house drifting over the lawn.

"What d'you think, Amy? Good idea?"

"Yeah, I suppose so."

"Great. I'll ask Dora to organise it tomorrow."

Amy looked up at him. "I suppose you and Hannah will *be* at the party?"

"We wouldn't miss it for the world."

He'd poured a glass of cold juice and was halfway out of the door with it. Amy said quickly, "Dad?"

"Yes, sweetheart?"

"What you said at breakfast. About wishing you had six weeks off."

"So I did."

"Have you planned a holiday?"

"D'you know, it's amazing you should mention it . . . "

"Oh?" Amy kept her head down. She drizzled olive oil on the salad, watched the raw spinach leaves gleam.

"It's exactly what we discussed over lunch. We thought while you're in Paris we could go to Wales. Just for a week. I wouldn't want you to be alone in the house . . . "

"I could always stay at Ruth's."

"No, a week will be fine. Hannah wants me to meet her parents in Cardiff. Then she and I can spend a few days walking in the mountains. Fresh air, exercise . . . "

"Just what the doctor ordered."

So now he's meeting her parents!

Dad laughed. "Really? You wouldn't mind? You know, if Hannah and I . . . "

It wouldn't matter much if I did.

"What'll we do with Tyler?"

"I'll ask Dora to have him. She'll spoil him rotten and he'll adore it. It'll give her a holiday too."

Better and better.

"That's settled, then." Amy picked up the salad bowl. "Could you tell Julian supper's ready?"

Amy watched Dad leave the kitchen. This afternoon, her plan had seemed far-fetched and ridiculous. Not any more . . .

Amy opens her wardrobe and takes out the new dress. It swishes against her.

"What d'you think?"

Ruth gasps. "It's *gorgeous*. It must've cost a fortune."

"Less than half price."

"Put it on."

Amy kicks off her trainers, strips off her T-shirt and jeans. Gently, she pulls the dress over her head. The silk rustles seductively.

"You don't think it's a bit over the top?"

"Nonsense. You look *fantastic*. I've never seen you in red before. Give us a twirl."

Amy twirls. The flared knee-length skirt lifts around her thighs.

"You'll need shoes to match . . . and to put your hair up."

Amy scoops it into a high ponytail. "Like that?"

"With a red ribbon, something to set it off. You'll look fabulous. 'Specially with that new sparkle in your eye."

"What new sparkle?" Amy pretends to adjust the scoop of the dress's neckline.

"You tell me."

Amy giggles. "If you must know, Christopher's coming to the party."

Ruth sits up on the bed. "Julian's friend? The one you met in Cambridge last year?"

"Yes," Amy says. "And I met him before, at Julian's school. When I was thirteen."

Ruth stares at her. "You never told me! Amy Grant, you're blushing! You're as red as your dress. You fancy him like mad. Come on, Miss I-Can't-Be-Bothered-with-Boys! Own up to Auntie Ruth."

Amy slides the dress off, sorry to part with it. She runs her fingers down its skirt, turns to look at Ruth.

"He's not a boy," she says. "He's twenty years old."

"Don't you think —" Ruth hesitates — "he might be a bit old for you?"

Amy starts to dance around the room in her underwear,

leaping and bounding, clapping her hands above her head, clicking her fingers to the beat of her body.

"*Old*? My Christopher? He's *perfect* . . . Just you wait and see!"

8

On Friday Amy wakes to the heavy pattering of rain.

She wrenches the curtains aside and opens the window. A warm summer wind batters the trees. Lupins and delphiniums sag their bright heads beneath the torrent. Fairy lights dangle from drenched branches, trying to hold on. Puddles collect on the terrace. A drove of starlings, blue-black and glittering, swoops noisily to drink.

At midday Julian says, "I'm going to collect Chris from Haslemere. Are you coming to the station with me?"

Amy's courage seeps away. "I'll wait here."

"Sure? We'll probably have a pub lunch on the way back."

"I've got tons of things to do for the party."

"Hmm . . . Bad luck, sis . . . Looks like it'll have to be indoors."

"Oh, *don't* say that."

Amy paces the house, unable to concentrate on anything.

She polishes the rows of glasses for the party, checks the caterers' list of food, which they'll deliver tomorrow.

She clears the hall of coats, muddy boots and junk mail.

She dashes out into the rain to pick pink and yellow roses, their petals cool and wet. She arranges them in the living room. She carries a vase of them upstairs, to the bedroom on the second floor where Chris will sleep. Their fragrance fills the air.

She puts blue candles in the holders on the dining-room table, fresh sandalwood soap in the downstairs loo. She throws away bundles of old newspapers, plumps the cushions, banishes Tyler's basket to the kitchen, cleans the stained-glass windows in the hall.

The house gleams.

Tyler sleeps on a window-seat dreaming of rabbits, his ears twitching.

Slowly, the rain eases, then stops. The sun struggles out from buxom purple clouds. Leaves drip.

Amy runs up to her room. She changes her shirt three times, finally deciding on a plain white blouse, unbuttoned at the neck. Her hair flows over her shoulders, long and loose. She puts on Burnt Sienna lipstick, but her hand shakes so much the colour smudges. Impatiently, she wipes it off.

When she hears Julian's car, she darts down the stairs and across the hall, flinging open the front door. Christopher climbs out of the car and stands beside Julian, who opens the boot and pulls out Chris's bag.

Amy swallows. Suddenly her voice is trapped.

Then, loudly, she calls, "Hi! Welcome to Terra Firma!"

Chris turns. He shades his eyes against the sun and looks at her.

He smiles.

Amy carries a tea tray on to the terrace. The garden smells damp and fresh. She pours the dark liquid, gives out the cups, trying to steady her hand.

China clinks.

Chris and Amy talk. Their words flow into and out of each other's, interweaving. They laugh. Their laughter floats upwards to the fairy lights. The garden steams beneath the heat of afternoon.

Tyler barks for attention. Amy throws him half a short-bread biscuit. He crunches it with gusto, then scampers to the end of the garden, begging for a walk.

The phone rings in the hall. Julian says, "I'll go."

For the first time, Amy and Chris are alone. She looks across at him. Her heart thrums in the river of quiet between them.

He leans forward. "So —" his hair catches the sunlight — "tomorrow. Who's coming to your party?"

"Lots of friends. From school and the local club. Dad and Hannah will be there."

"Jules told me about her."

"Yeah . . . And Aunt Charlotte . . . and neighbours, people from the village . . . "

Chris edges his chair closer to Amy's. "I thought you might have a boyfriend."

Amy thinks of Pete Franklin. "No. The boys at school are, well, *boys!*" She bites her lip. "Nothing special. Nothing romantic . . . But what about you? You must be spoilt for choice. All those glamorous students, the girls you act with?"

He grins. "I haven't been short of offers. But nobody's really taken my fancy. There's no one I –"

Julian returns to the terrace. "Just somebody for Dad."

Chris straightens his back. "I was sorry you couldn't come to see me in *Cyrano de Bergerac*," he says more loudly than necessary.

"So was I." Amy collects the teacups. "My exams got in the way of everything."

"But they went well, yeah?"

Amy catches the half-smile in Chris's eyes. It implies: I'm merely making idle chat. There are other things I'd much rather say to you.

She says hurriedly, "The exams were fine. No problem."

Julian says, "Chris was brilliant as Cyrano. Did I tell you? An agent from London came to see him. Met him backstage and signed him on the spot. We may yet see his name in lights."

In my head, Christopher's name has always been in lights.

"He's *gorgeous*," Ruth said.

She'd met Chris in the hall as she flew upstairs to Amy's room.

Amy laughed. "See? What did I tell you?"

"When did he arrive?"

"Yesterday. It's been fantastic. We had supper with Dad and Hannah. I hardly noticed her!"

Ruth laughed. "Poor Hannah!"

"And then we took Tyler for a walk, and this morning Aunt Charlotte arrived and we left her and Dad together, and Julian took us for a drive to show Chris the countryside and we had lunch at the Bishop's Table in Farnham . . ." Amy paused for breath. "It's been the best."

Ruth sat down on the bed. "I can't believe it."

"He makes me laugh. He's got the most beautiful speaking voice."

"You're well and truly smitten!"

"Yes." Amy flopped down next to Ruth. "I'm crazy about him."

"I'd begun to wonder."

"Whether I'd ever feel like this? Well, I do." Amy blushed. "I want to be with him all the time, listening to him, looking at him. I could hardly get to sleep last night, knowing he was upstairs."

Ruth said quietly, "That's great, Amy. And happy birthday. You look beautiful."

"Are you sure the dress is OK?"

"It's stunning." Ruth rustled in her bag. "Here. These are from Mum and me."

"Ruth! You shouldn't have."

Amy unwrapped a pair of earrings in softly glinting pearl. She caught her breath. "I don't know what to say . . . Thank you!" She clipped them on. "What d' you think?"

"The perfect finishing touch. Are you ready, birthday girl?"

"I'm ready . . . Here I come!"

Ruth rushed down to join Eddie, who'd begun to organise the music.

Amy stood for a moment on the landing, listening to the buzz of happy voices. And suddenly two others, dark, bitter, coming from Dad's bedroom. Her heart leapt. Perhaps Dad was arguing with Hannah, telling her to get out of his life?

"But you *promised* me."

Amy froze. Aunt Charlotte was in Dad's bedroom. Her voice sounded thick and smeary, as if she'd been crying.

"I'm sorry, Lottie," Dad said, low, urgent, as if he were trying to get rid of her. "I'm grateful to you for all your help, all your —"

"Grateful!" Amy heard a slap. "You're a lying *pig*, William Grant. Why d'you think I've bothered to love you all these years?"

"I've no idea."

"You *promised* you'd marry me, after a decent time had passed, after Lauren . . . "

"My dear Lottie, I did nothing of the kind."

"You mean, after all these *years* of being so discreet and hiding my real feelings from the children, making sure they never found us together . . . "

Amy walked past the door and stiffly down the stairs, her heart thudding against the silk of her dress.

Good God. Dad and Aunt Charlotte. So that's *why she kept on coming here, year after year . . . All that comforting she did when Mum died . . . I remember now . . . Always the first to say, "Don't cry, dear William, don't cry."*

Chris met her at the bottom of the stairs.

"Hey!" he said. "Just look at Jules's little sister now!"

*

96

The downstairs rooms thronged with guests. Tyler, banished to the kitchen, chewed miserably on a bone. Eddie's music filled the house, floated to the starry summer sky. Plates of food scented the terrace table.

The fairy lights had triumphantly survived the deluge. Now they swung and glittered from the trees, painting the garden magical rainbow colours.

Aunt Charlotte handed out drinks from a tray, her eyes dark with rage whenever she glanced at Dad and Hannah laughing together. Later, Dad said Aunt Charlotte wasn't feeling well and had driven back to London.

Amy stared at him with hardened eyes.

Dad insisted on making a speech.

In the moment of silence before he spoke, Amy remembered Mum's funeral, how they had toasted "Lauren", her own wretched muteness – and Aunt Charlotte's comforting presence.

The room darkened at the memory.

"I wanted to say thank you, to everyone, for being here. And happy birthday to my best and darling daughter, who looks so beautiful tonight. We wish you the happiest year of your life." He raised his glass. "Amy. Happy birthday."

"Amy! Happy birthday!"

Amy's eyes filled with tears. "Thanks, Dad."

Christopher says, "I've got a present for you." He grips Amy's hand.

His touch charges through her body. "I didn't expect . . . "

"Come into the garden, away from all these people. I want to give it to you before your birthday's several days old!"

He slides an arm around her waist. They cross the terrace and the lawn, wander through the sweet dampness of the rose garden to the edge of the Common. A curved sliver of moon hangs like a midnight jewel, parting the clouds around it.

"Here." He gives her a small flat parcel.

Amy tears at the wrapping. It's a book, slim in its leather binding. "Chris! But I can't see what it is!"

He chuckles. "It's an edition of *Shakespeare's Sonnets*. I love them. I wanted you to have a copy."

"*Thank* you."

"Hold it carefully. I've put something inside to mark my favourite."

"Which one is it?"

"Aha! You'll have to open it and see in the quiet of your room."

Amy runs her fingers over the smooth leather.

"Amy?"

"Yes." She looks into his face, half hidden in the shadows.

"I think you know how I feel about you." Chris moves a step closer. His eyes glitter in the moonlight. "Ever since the cricket match." The tips of his fingers touch her bare shoulders, stroke them like the wings of a butterfly. Her skin sparkles. "Ever since last year. Do you remember?" Closer still. "That afternoon on the river?"

Amy feels the warmth of Chris's body against her, the crispness of his shirt beneath her hands. "Of course I remember."

"I've thought about you such a lot." His lips brush her hair. "I wondered —"

Amy stiffens. Suddenly the only thing she can hear is the murmur of two other voices. One of them laughs. It's Hannah. Hannah and Dad.

Nausea rises up Amy's throat and into her mouth. She pulls out of Chris's arms. "I'm sorry," she says abruptly. "I have to go in."

Amy runs back across the garden.

She pushes through the guests, races up to her room. She stands with her back to the door, her legs trembling, her hair tumbling around her shoulders. Her heart beats like pounding rain.

Chris will think I don't want him. I want him so much I can hardly stand up. But the thought of Dad and Hannah kissing makes me feel sick. It's supposed to be Chris and me under those fairy lights, not Dad and Hannah.

It's my *garden. Mum's and mine.*

Amy sinks on to the bed, looks down at the book in her hand. Under the light, the leather binding gleams a luxuriant crimson. Slowly she opens it, reads the inscription:

For Amy, now you are sixteen. With my love, Christopher

In the centre of the book lies a carefully crushed, pale yellow rose, its stem stripped of thorns. Chris must have chosen it from the ones she'd put on his bedside table. Underneath the rose lies Sonnet 116. The words blur into each other as she reads:

> *Let me not to the marriage of true minds*
> *Admit impediments, love is not love*
> *Which alters when it alteration finds,*
> *Nor bends with the remover to remove.*
> *O, no, it is an ever-fixed mark*
> *That looks on tempest and is never shaken*
> *It is the star to every wand'ring bark,*

Whose worth's unknown although his height be taken,
Love's not Time's fool, though rosy lips and cheeks
Within his bending sickle's compass come,
Love alters not with his brief hours and weeks,
But bears it out even to the edge of doom:
If this be error and upon me proved
I never writ, nor no man ever loved.

With infinite care, Amy closes the flower into its page. Hot tears burn behind her eyes.

She lies awake, staring into the dark, filled with a confusion of feelings. Wanting to talk to Aunt Charlotte, to confide in her — to hear her story. Anger at Dad. Resentment of Hannah. Longing for Christopher, for the stroke of his fingers, the touch of his lips. Bitter remorse that she ran away.

She hears Chris and Julian come up the stairs, hears them mutter, "Good night," on the landing. She wills Chris to tap at her door, whisper, "Amy? Are you awake?"

Instead, silence throbs into the darkness. An owl hoots, mournful, complaining. In the garden, cats spit fresh animosities. On the Common, the foxes scream for food.

Nobody taps at the door.

Her bedside clock shows two, three, four. She hears something creak on the landing. Perhaps it's Chris, not sure which door to tap on?

She slips out of bed and opens her door a fraction.

Hannah stands in the doorway of Dad's room, blows him a kiss, whispers, "See you tonight, darling. Love you." She vanishes down the stairs, trailing lily-of-the-valley.

Tyler growls from his basket.

Hannah murmurs, "Good dog, Tyler. It's only me."

The front door opens and closes. Hannah revs her car and drives away.

Amy slumps back on to her damp, tangled sheets. She falls instantly into the pit of sleep.

When she wakes, sunlight splashes fiercely on her pillow. The clock says half-past eleven. Amy stares at it. Memories of yesterday flood back.

She sits up with a start.

A piece of paper has been pushed under her door.

She leaps out of bed, scrabbles at it.

Dear Amy

Jules and I have left for Perugia. We didn't want to wake you. Thank you for a lovely party. If anything I said last night offended

*you, I can only say I must have misread all the signs. I'm desperately
sorry.*

Take care of yourself.

Love Christopher

"You've been crying."

Ruth stood in the doorway. She pulled Amy into the
house.

"Cup of tea? Come into the kitchen. Everybody's gone for
a Sunday afternoon walk but I'm knackered after last night.
What's wrong?"

Amy told her. First about Dad and Aunt Charlotte. Then
Dad and Hannah. Then Chris. She pulled Chris's note out of
her pocket. "Look. That's the last I'll probably ever hear
from him."

Ruth glanced at it. "Don't be so melodramatic. Why don't
you write to him and explain? I'm sure he'll understand."

"Where do I write? I haven't got an address in Perugia,
and even if I had, by the time it arrives he'll probably have
moved on."

"Hasn't Julian left you an address? You must have *some* idea
where they've gone . . . Here, drink this."

Amy clutched the mug of tea. "Maybe Dad knows. I feel
such a fool. What was I thinking of, running off like that?"

"You'd had a shock."

"Too right. It's the last thing I expected, Dad and Hannah snogging like teenagers!"

Ruth giggled.

"It's not funny."

"Sorry. Though it is romantic, isn't it? Your dad finding true love again."

Amy said venomously, "True love? True nothing!" She gulped the burning tea. "They went to bed together. I saw her leaving Dad's room at four o'clock."

"I think you should give him a break."

"Why *should* I?"

"Because Hannah's better than Aunt Charlotte! He's got a girlfriend and he's obviously head over heels. So they're sleeping together. Wouldn't it be odd if they weren't?"

"It's all right for you." Amy's hand shook. A dollop of tea flopped on her jeans, spreading a dark puddle, stinging her thigh. "You can look at it from the outside. He's my *dad*. Or should I say, he *was* my dad? It's like I've lost him to a stranger."

"He'll *always* be your dad."

"And now, in the space of one glorious weekend, I've lost Christopher too."

9

"Well, sweetheart," Dad says cheerfully.

He'd slicked his hair back from his forehead after his shower. Amy notices with alarm it makes him look ten years younger. He also looks thinner. All that stupid cycling, that cavorting on the trampoline, are obviously paying off.

"Just you and me together again for Monday morning breakfast . . . How nice."

"You could say that." Amy stuffs a forkful of scrambled eggs into her mouth. It tastes disgusting. *I must've sploshed half a sea of salt into this by mistake.*

"What *do* you mean?"

"Only that I'm sure *you'd* like there to be three of us."

"You mean you miss Jules?" Dad sounds relieved. "So do I. And Christopher – charming lad."

Amy tries to ignore the way her heart leaps into her mouth at the mention of Chris. "I mean you wish your darling Hannah was right here beside you."

"I *beg* your pardon!" Dad splutters into his juice.

"Seeing as how you're practically joined at the hip," Amy

continues in a deadpan voice, "I'm amazed you haven't already asked her to move in."

Dad gulps. His face, Amy sees with delight, has flushed a dark red. "There's no need to be offensive."

She glares at him. "I think there's *every* need."

"My friendship with Hannah —"

"It's a bit more than *friendship*, Dad."

"That's nothing to do with you!"

"Isn't it?" Amy's heart thuds with indignation. "Snogging in the garden at my birthday party? Sleeping with Hannah when Jules and Chris and me were upstairs, across the landing? Just *friends*, are we, Dad?"

He flings down his serviette. "Look here, Amy. I will not have you talking to me like that. Understand?"

"No, I *don't*." She clenches her fists. "You've started behaving like a besotted teenager!"

"A *what?*"

"After all those brilliant years with Mum . . . How *dare* you betray her?"

Dad stares at her. Thin lines etch the corners of his eyes. "You've no idea what you're talking about." His face darkens. "I was never, for one single solitary moment, disloyal or unfaithful to your mother. It was she who . . . " He turns his head away.

"Who what?"

"Never mind. I've already said too much."

"You've told me nothing."

"That's how it's going to stay." Dad runs a hand through his hair. It flops into its usual untidy zigzag. "I'm not saying any more, not one word." He stands up. "If you'll excuse me, my patients are waiting."

"Sure, your patients. Don't let me keep you from them. Talk to *them*, do you, Dad?"

"You know I do."

"Then why don't you talk to *me*?"

Dad turns from the door. "I'll say this to you, and then the subject is closed." The sprightly vigour has drained from his body. "Mum was a wonderful woman, a good wife and a great mother." He hesitates. "But she wasn't perfect, Amy. Don't make out she was some kind of saint."

Amy shivers. Once again, Ruth's words ring in her head: *"You put your mum on a bit of a pedestal."*

"I loved her." Amy's voice sounds thin and feeble, her palms feel clammy with sweat.

"So did I. With all my heart." Dad chokes over the words. "But if you think that's going to stop me loving Hannah, you're *very* much mistaken."

*

Amy walked up and down the hill of Guildford High Street. She took a deep breath and dashed into the bank. She used her cashcard for the first time, reciting her pin number to herself, staring anxiously at the screen's instructions, prodding nervously at the buttons.

The notes smelt stale. She stuffed them into her bag, glanced guiltily over her shoulder, whizzed out to the street as if the bank were on fire.

I don't know what I'm making such a fuss about. It's my money, my allowance. I'll spend it how I want.

She headed straight for the travel agent's, pushed at the door, surprised and relieved that she was the only customer. A pale-faced young man with spots and greasy hair gave her a weary grin.

Amy flicked her hair over her shoulder. "A friend of mine," she said carefully, "wants to go to Florence. She's asked me to get her some details. She wants to go in August, in a fortnight's time. On Sunday 12th August, travelling back the following Saturday, the 18th. Could you tell me how much it'll cost?"

"It depends where she wants to stay." The man looked instantly more interested, as if he could see another fat commission in his payslip. "Plain or fancy?"

"Plain. Clean and decent. And safe. But no frills. Bed and breakfast will do."

"Right." He jabbed a stubby finger at his computer. "I assume she'll be flying direct to Florence? If so, she'll have to leave from Gatwick. If she wants to fly from Heathrow, she'll have to go to Rome or Zurich and change planes."

Amy's stomach clenched with fright. "Gatwick direct."

"With a door-to-door service? Does she want an airline car to pick her up?"

Amy thought rapidly. If she used a local taxi firm, the driver might recognise her, wonder — and gossip about — why she was travelling alone. Buses on a Sunday morning would be non-existent. If she wanted to escape incognito, she'd better do it properly. "Yes, please. Door to door."

He screwed up his eyes against the computer's glare. "There's one seat for Sunday the 11th, leaving on the afternoon flight at two-fifteen. Shall I reserve it?"

"I need to talk to my friend."

"I'll hold it for you until noon. After that, it's first come, first served." He glanced around the empty shop. "We get very busy this time of year."

Amy perched uncomfortably in Starbucks, on a stool by the window, trying to scrape up enough courage to go back to the travel agent's and admit the ticket was for her. The froth on her cooling cappuccino sank to a thin scum.

She had the money, the details, the opportunity. She had the motive. She'd bought a map of Florence, a guidebook to Italy and a rapid learner's paperback: *Speak Italian in a Week*. She'd be an idiot to lose her bottle now.

She gazed enviously at the carefree shoppers in their sunhats, shorts and floppy shirts. They seemed so confident, so sure where they were going.

What if she flew to Florence and something went wrong? Nobody would know where she was for a whole week, not Dad, not Julian, not Ruth. She couldn't tell Ruth. If she did, she'd have to tell her about Marcello. Or invent some improbable story that Ruth would see through like a shot.

If she was going, it'd have to be a secret flight. Taking the risk. The real Houdini.

She sipped at her cold coffee, grimaced, pushed the cup aside.

It was no good.

Too many things might go wrong. She'd get lost at the airport or in Florence. She'd be mugged, lose all her money, her tickets, be unable to get home. The plane might crash. Nobody would be able to identify her. Everyone would think she'd vanished off the face of the earth, run away from home because she didn't want to be with Dad.

The whole idea had been ludicrous. She'd never find

Marcello — and even if she did, what on earth would she say to him? Did she really intend to wave a battered old postcard under his nose, demanding to know whether he'd written it and why?

She could think of nothing more undignified. He'd never admit to anything. He'd probably forgotten who Mum was. He'd have a wife and six children by now. He'd think she was some crazy little English kid.

The week would be a waste of time and money.

She stood up. End of story. She'd go straight home and tear up that wretched card. Grit her teeth and go to France with Mrs Boring Baxter. She flung her bag over her shoulder.

A woman pushed into Starbucks, bumping against her. The scent of lily-of-the-valley filled the air.

"Amy!" Hannah wore an immaculate ice-blue trouser suit with a floaty chiffon scarf. Her hair had been freshly washed and cut. Amy felt dowdy and dull. "What a lovely surprise! May I join you?"

"I'm just leaving."

"Another ten minutes won't hurt. I've got the day off. The freedom's quite gone to my head."

"I'm meeting someone in half an hour."

"That gives us plenty of time." Hannah guided Amy

towards an empty table. "I've been meaning to have a chat with you for ages."

Amy plonked herself into a chair, squashing her bag beneath it so that Hannah wouldn't spot the books on Italy.

Triumphantly, Hannah brought over two fruit smoothies. "There now! Much better than another slug of caffeine." She slid gracefully into a chair. "Isn't this fun?"

Amy bit her lip.

"I wanted to say a special thank-you for asking me to your birthday party. I'm getting to know lots of the villagers in a professional capacity, but it's great once in a while not to wear my doctor's hat!"

Amy filled her mouth with the smoothie. Banana and lemon sorbet, a weird mixture, surprisingly delicious, heavy and refreshing. *I'll let her chatter on for another ten minutes. Then I'll get up and go straight home.*

"I also wanted to say," the hazel eyes flickered, "William's told me all about your mum and the accident. I'm so proud of you." Her voice darkened. "It's not easy, it it?"

"What isn't?" Amy asked rudely.

"Coping with life when you've lost somebody you love."

"How would *you* know?"

Hannah dipped her head. "I was engaged to a medical student. Eight years ago."

In spite of herself, Amy was intrigued. "What happened?"

"He was killed in a road accident. We never had a chance to say goodbye. It took me two years to recover." Hannah's eyes sparked with tears. "I don't talk about it." She sipped her drink. A thin line of banana froth clung to her lipsticked mouth. "I haven't even told William. That's how private it is."

"So why tell me?"

"Because I want you to know I'm on your side. It must be hard, me being around, after having your dad to yourself. I don't want to come between you, I honestly don't."

Some hope. You've come between us good and proper.

She looked Hannah in the eyes. "Do you love him?"

Hannah blushed. "It would be hard *not* to. I don't fall in love easily. After Jack died, I never thought . . . " She fiddled with her scarf. "It's partly why I went to Africa."

Amy drank to the bottom of the liquid. Her stomach felt as if she'd eaten a three-course meal.

"I wanted to get away from everything. It's extraordinary the difference it can make."

Amy put down her glass. "You think so?"

"I *know* so. Going off on your own gives you an incredible sense of independence. Puts everything in perspective. All the snarls you get trapped in are sorted, just like that."

"Really?"

"Best thing I ever did. Before Africa, I'd always belonged to someone else. I was their daughter or their sister or their aunt. Their lover. Their student or their lodger. Africa let me breathe. Gave me the freedom to be myself.

"At first, it's frightening. You think, God, I'm on my own. I've made the wrong choice, it's too late to turn back. But then your courage takes over and you find yourself . . . Do you understand?"

"Yeah," Amy said slowly. "I think I do." She glanced at her watch. She had five minutes to get to the travel agent's.

"Thanks for the drink," she said. "I've got to go."

Amy checked the contents of her leather bag yet again. Passport, tickets, traveller's cheques, euros, the map of Florence, the guidebook, *Speak Italian in a Week*. Marcello's card. And her beloved copy of *Shakespeare's Sonnets*.

Guiltily she squashed the bag behind her desk.

Yesterday Dad had asked her whether she minded if he and Hannah left for Cardiff on Friday evening.

"It'll mean we'll have two clear weekends and the week between," he said. "Dora's agreed to have Tyler. He'll go off with her on Friday morning."

"That's fine," Amy said quickly. "I'll spend Saturday with Ruth. We're leaving early on Sunday to catch the Eurostar."

"You must be looking forward to Paris. It's such a romantic city."

"Oh, I am," Amy said blankly. "Very much indeed."

Amy waves them goodbye, stands silently in the doorway, shuts the front door behind her. The house feels eerily quiet. Tyler's scampering feet echo in her ears. The wind sighs in the firs.

She picks up the phone.

"Ruth, it's me."

"Hi! Coming for lunch tomorrow?"

"That's what I've rung about. I'm not feeling well, and I thought, seeing as how we're off on Sunday, maybe I'd better stay in bed."

"What's the matter?"

"A cracking headache and I feel sick. I haven't eaten anything all day. The thought of food makes me feel like throwing up."

"Shall I come over and play nurse?"

"No. I'll be fine . . . I'll ring you tomorrow."

"Ruth, it's me."

"How are you?"

Amy gives her voice a feeble tremor. "A lot worse."

"Have you been sick?" Ruth sounds worried.

"I'm afraid I have."

"You'd better see a doctor."

"I've just spoken to Dr Martin at Dad's surgery. He said he'll pop in this evening. But it's bad news about the trip. He says I've got gastric flu and I can't travel."

"I'm coming straight round."

"No, don't. I won't let you in. It could be contagious."

"I'm not going to Paris without you."

"Of *course* you are." Amy's heart thuds with sudden alarm. "You'll only be away a week."

"But I'll miss you so much . . . You'll be all on your own."

"The way I feel at the moment, that's exactly what I *want* to be . . . Honestly, Ruth, I'll be perfectly OK. Dr Martin will give me something. I've got to rest and drink plenty of water."

Ruth says doubtfully, "If you're sure . . . "

"Quite sure. I'll ring Mrs Baxter, let her know I won't be able to come."

"She'll be so upset."

It's too late now to change my mind. I've got to see it through.

"You'll have to tell me about it the minute you get back."

116

"I'll buy you something wonderful from the Champs-Elysées . . . Get better soon."

"I will," says Amy. "Have a brilliant time."

She clicks back the phone.

She stares blankly around the hall: at the sunlight filtering through the stained-glass windows, the vase of roses on the table, the raincoats hanging from their wooden rail.

Everything seems motionless, as if it is listening with incredulity to the web of lies she has so deftly spun and told.

She races upstairs to Mum's study, stands looking at her portrait. Her heart beats fast as the wings of a moth trapped in a circle of light.

"I'm doing this for you, Mum. You understand why, don't you? Why I've told everyone a different story. Why I must do this on my own."

She swallows.

"I want to clear your name. I want to find Marcello. I need to know if he was on the Common that morning."

She tilts her head to look Mum clearly in the eyes. Those extraordinary pale grey-green eyes that seem to flicker with love.

"I think someone killed you. And I can't rest until I've found out who it was."

10

Gatwick bustles with nervous noise.

It is a shock, after the stillness of early-morning Surrey, where sheep graze, Sunday bells toll and most people still sleep. At the airport, every handrail throbs and hums.

Amy stares out of the window of her plane at the ones about to fly. They sprawl on the runway like giant fish on wheels, only their flashing heartbeat lights betraying the life within.

Her plane's vast engine churns. The plane thrums, roars, moves forward and, with a great song and dance, lifts into the sky: through purple banks of thunderclouds, away and above them, over southern England and the green and golden patchwork handkerchiefs of France. She is trapped in a world of sky and blotting-paper cloud, seat belts, orange juice and professional politeness.

She opens her bag, strokes the soft leather binding of *Shakespeare's Sonnets* for reassurance. Next to her, an Italian businessman consumes *Corriere della Sera*, rustling the pages, grunting impatiently. Amy looks out of the window. She can see nothing but a world of impenetrable cloud.

A meal is served: hot pasties with mushrooms smelling of seaweed, stale almond biscuits, a soft roll with cream cheese. Amy drinks some tea but she cannot eat. After a tactful half-hour, a stewardess removes the tray.

Amy closes her eyes. She is haunted by random memories of Mum: the soft frills of a pale-green silk dress Mum had worn for her first book launch; seeing her lying in a hammock on the terrace, crying over a novel she'd been reading; cooking a turkey in their steamy kitchen, the snow drifting on the lawn, neither of them ever dreaming it would be Mum's last Christmas.

Fitfully, Amy dozes into sleep. The pilot's instruction to *Please fasten your seat belts* jolts her awake. As the plane dips towards Amerigo Vespucci Airport, she forces her mind into the immediate moment, sets her watch forward by one hour.

The Sunday bells toll in Florence too. Amy collects her luggage, nervously searches for her driver. GRANT says the placard. *"Grazie,"* Amy squeaks. The Fiat's driver whisks her away at grumpy hair-raising speed on what feels unnervingly like the wrong side of the road.

Her small hotel on the Via Guiccardini is discreet and serviceable. In her featureless room on the first floor, Amy opens the window on to a small iron balcony. It overlooks a courtyard of crumbling stone. On a washing line, hanging beneath a row of brown shutters, white shirts, aprons and a chef's hat bake in the heat. The smells of olive oil, fish and garlic drift from the kitchen below. Hunger clutches at her stomach.

She flings off her clothes, steps into a cool shower. Wrapped in a towel, she spreads her map of Florence on the narrow bed and tries to get her bearings.

If she walks out of the hotel and turns left, she will reach the Ponte Vecchio. Crossing the bridge will lead her into the centre of the city. After she has eaten — a risotto, perhaps, or ravioli with cheese — she will begin . . . What? Her search? No, it is more important than that. Her quest. She will put on her sleuthing hat and become Detective Amy Grant.

Don't forget, she tells herself firmly ten minutes later, as she stands at the hotel doorway. *You're here on a mission. Don't get sucked into the museums, the churches, the galleries. However beautiful, they won't help you find Marcello. That's what you're here to do.*

For two days Amy walked.

Into and out of the centre of Florence. Up and down the narrow, bustling streets. To and from the station. Past a hundred *pizzeria* and small shops selling exquisite leather shoes and bags, into and out of the elegant squares.

She walked round the outside of the Duomo until she felt dizzy at its size. She walked over the bridges and along the River Arno. She walked until her mouth felt dry as a bone and her arms and cheeks flamed in the relentless sun. *Better keep out of the sun. Ruth will never believe I've stayed at home!*

The early mornings were the best, before the heat began to bite and while the narrow streets were empty. Shopkeepers brushed their soft straw brooms *swish, swish* across their slabs of cobbled pavement. On the Ponte Vecchio, jewellers polished the wooden casings of their shops, opened and cleaned their windows, stretched long arms to place each glittering stone on its cushion with immaculate precision.

Beneath the bridges, the River Arno slept motionless, a mirror to the thick blocks of flats against its bank, echoing the pinks and yellows of their walls, the greens and browns of their shuttered windows, the summer blooms in their roof gardens.

By eleven o'clock the squares had filled with the crush and jabber of guides and groups, the click of cameras, the squeal of mobile phones; the streets with the honk of cars and the angry buzz of motorbikes.

Amy walked doggedly, persistently, looking for clues, listening to likely voices, opening guidebooks on Tuscan villas and closing them again, scanning the postcards at the stalls on each street corner. Photos of Michelangelo's *David* stared out at her from every angle, his flesh cool, grey, haughty, accusing.

"You can't find Marcello, can you?" *David* seemed to say as Amy stared up at a copy of the statue in the Palazzo Vecchio. "I know where he is, of course." The closed mouth curled its lovely lips. "But it's my special secret and I'm not telling *you*."

On Tuesday afternoon, she escaped the city's noise for two hours by climbing the steep pebbly paths of the Giardino de Boboli and sitting among its formal green lawns, staring into space. She read Chris's favourite sonnet for the umpteenth time. The petals of the faded yellow rose bleached beneath the sun.

Amy eats supper alone again that night.

A group of boys at a nearby table try to chat her up. She fends them off as politely as she can, but they persist. Blushing and furious, she stands up, pays her bill at the counter, pushes out of the café. The boys think it's hilarious.

She stands outside, trembling. Trying to still the beating of her heart, she fills her lungs with the night air. The whiff of drains catches the back of her throat.

She gasps. She remembers . . .

She is only nine.

She is mute.

She is standing in the hall, waiting for Dad. Tyler barks and flaps around her legs. They have to leave soon. They are having tea with Frances, their vicar, and they shouldn't be late because other people from the village will be there too.

Now that Dad hasn't got Mum to organise him, even though Aunt Charlotte does her best, things aren't the same, he gets into muddles, he is often late.

She sidles into the kitchen and looks round the door. Dad is hurling food from the freezer into a rubbish bag. All the meals Mum had cooked and put in there. Dad is flinging them away.

He sees her come into the kitchen.

He looks up at her.

His face is black with rage.

On Wednesday morning Amy woke with a resounding headache. Her temples throbbed, her body felt stiff and sore. In the shower, a blister on her heel cried with pain. She limped across to a café for a cappuccino and a crunchy sandwich. They gave her comfort. A *farmacia* sold her a packet of plasters. Once again she crossed the Ponte Vecchio and passed the long Uffizi galleries.

An artist sat at the bottom of the narrow flight of steps, sketching the head of a girl. The model gazed solemnly at him, her dark curls tumbling to her shoulders. She looked so like Ruth that for an instant Amy's heart leapt.

Of course, it wasn't Ruth. The girl's face was fuller, her body smaller. Amy bit the inside of her lip and walked on, shaking with homesickness. She missed Ruth and Julian; she imagined Dad and Hannah walking hand in hand in the Welsh mountains; she wanted to hear Tyler's welcoming bark. She longed for the sound of Chris's voice, for the thrill of his touch – and wondered bitterly whether she'd ever feel it again.

Despondently, feeling more alone than ever as the expectant queues for the Uffizi gathered like a swarm of bees, she walked towards the Duomo Santa Maria del Fiore. This time, she went in. Or rather, she felt sucked in, at last, to its gigantic heart.

Inside the cathedral, the air is warm and grey. The scale of the place is monumental. Beneath the soaring heights of the cupola Amy feels like an inconsequential beetle. The swirling echoes of a million prayers murmur in her ears.

A bell clangs through the quiet. Two priests in apple-green surplices begin a short service against one of the marble altars.

Amy crouches on a polished wooden bench beside a massive wall. She stares up at the light filtering through the glow of a miraculous stained-glass window.

She takes stock.

I'm getting nowhere. I'm walking the skin off my feet for nothing. There must be a thousand Marcellos in Florence and not one of them is mine. He's probably gone to some wonderful beach somewhere and even now he's swimming in the sea.

I wish I were in the sea. Or walking on Ludshott Common in the wind and rain. I wish I could feel cool again. I'm suffocating here, and it's only Wednesday.

Amy stands up. She moves restlessly round the cathedral, beneath the flicker of votive candles, into and out of the dimness, willing the sanctity of the place to give her inspiration. Instead, it makes her feel so insignificant that her courage seeps away.

I could go to Paris and meet up with Ruth. I wonder whether I could catch a train from Florence that would take me straight there? That's a brilliant idea. Mrs Baxter would welcome me with open arms, slot me straight back into her schedules.

I need never tell her I'd been to Florence. I could pretend I'd recovered from gastric flu and decided to join them. It'd be so good to talk to Ruth again.

Fighting against the knowledge that she is giving up the quest, that her plans have come to nothing, that she lacks grit and determination, despising herself, deflated, irritated, Amy pushes out, through the cathedral door and into the oven of heat.

That's what I'll do. You're safe, Marcello. You can rest in peace. Just like Mum.

Halfway along the Via Panzani, on her way to the station to find out about trains to Paris, Amy stopped at a café. She sat with a glass of iced grapefruit juice, gulping at the liquid as if she had survived a week in the desert.

At the next table, two Americans talked at the tops of their voices.

"Yesterday was the best," the woman said. "It was so great to escape the heat of this city. Mom warned us about coming in August."

"It sure was marvellous." Her companion sipped his beer. "That Fiesole's so green. It's like it absorbs the sun."

"And that Maurizio, wasn't he charming?"

"You mean Marco?"

"Do I? Marco doesn't sound right. Wait a minute. What *was* his name? Mauro? Got it! Marcello, that's his name."

"Great guy. And the work he's done to that place!"

"Took him years and it's still not finished."

"Sure, but with a villa like that, the work's never done. You just go on and on."

Amy could bear it no longer. Clutching the icy glass, she bent towards them. "Excuse me, I hope you don't think I'm poking my nose in, but I couldn't help overhearing . . . You've been to a villa in Fiesole?"

"Sure we have, honey." The woman's pudgy fingers scrabbled in her bag, dragged out a postcard. "Here's a photo. Take a look. Doesn't do it justice."

Amy looked down at a dazzling hillside landscape. The back of the photo held the caption she'd been searching for: *The Italian Gardens of the Villa Galanti, copyright Marcello Galanti.*

"Well worth a visit." The man drained his beer. "Worth every cent."

"Keep the photo." The woman hoisted herself out of her chair. "Phone number's on the back."

Amy looked up at her. "Thank you so much."

"You're more than welcome. You have to book in advance. Their minibus collects you at the station. Like my hubby says, it ain't cheap, but it's worth every cent. Good luck, honey. Hope you get to see it. They're rushed off their feet this time of year."

Amy pushed against the crowds back to her hotel, the photograph of the Villa Galanti slippery hot in her hand.

In her room, panting, she picked up the phone.

"*Pronto?* I would like to visit your gardens today, now, this afternoon, as soon as I can," she jabbered to the cool voice at the end of the line. She closed her eyes, trying to imagine where the voice came from: an elegant air-conditioned office overlooking the hills, a small polished desk, a neat pile of letters.

"I am sorry, *signorina*, but we are fully booked for the rest of August." The voice crisply signed her off.

Panic gripped Amy. "You can't be." She leaned against the wall. "I've come all the way from England to see you. It's most important. I have to leave Florence on Saturday . . . Please."

"I am sorry to disappoint you. Perhaps you could return next year? Our minibus, it collects our guests and it holds only twelve people. Strictly only six times a day. We have been fully booked since the end of June—"

"There's only one of me," Amy cut in desperately. "Can't

you somehow squeeze me in? Please. I'll do anything, pay you anything you want."

There was a short, rather hostile, pause. "One moment, *signorina*."

The line went dead. Amy shook the phone as if she were trying to revive a dying snake. The phone buzzed into life. Italian voices rattled to each other.

"*Pronto?* Are you still there?"

Amy's knees gave way; she slumped on to the bed. "Yes, I'm still here."

"We have had a cancellation, *signorina*." The voice warmed by a fraction. "Two of our guests, they telephone us just now, they are delayed in New York. They were booked for the third minibus tomorrow morning, at eleven-thirty. Is that convenient?"

Through the shutters, a filter of golden light filled Amy's shadowy room. "That's fantastic." She stared down at the photograph, startled to notice it lay crumpled in her fist. "Thank you so much."

"*Prego, signorina*. You will please pay our driver at the station."

"Of course."

"And now, may I have your name for our records?"

"My name?"

Amy thought fast. What if Marcello checked through the lists at the start of each day? It was essential she take him completely unawares.

She said quietly into the mouth of the snake, "My name is Ruth Manning."

And she spelt out the surname, slowly and clearly, so there could be no possible misunderstanding.

11

Amy is relieved when the sounds of dawn – the creak of plumbing, voices calling in the courtyard, birds testing their first tentative chirps – allow her to slither out of bed. She has hardly slept but she feels refreshed, almost feather-headed.

She stands in the shower, washes her hair, dries and brushes it until it crackles beneath her hands. She pulls on a straight, white, sleeveless cotton dress, a white sunhat and her best sandals, praying their straps will leave the healing blister alone.

She reaches the station early, paces among the crowds, finally spots a white minibus winding through the traffic. It is marked *The Villa Galanti*. The driver bows, murmurs his name, "Umberto", ticks *Ruth Manning* off his list and takes her euros. He wears a pale suit and a handlebar moustache. He reminds Amy of a character from an old movie who has had a colourful past he would prefer to forget.

The rest of the group – Americans and a young Japanese couple whose hands are glued together – arrive *en masse*. The minibus lurches forward, wins an argument with a coach and triumphantly swings on to the road: round the rusty curve of railway, past dour blocks of flats, out on to the wider, tree-lined streets.

A signpost says FIESOLE. Amy squashes her face against the window. The landscape changes dramatically. The shops and town houses thin out and disappear. In their place stand large pink villas surrounded by lush gardens; groves of olive trees, their leaves a pale grey-green. They remind Amy of the colour of Mum's eyes.

The road begins to climb, steeply, and then steeper still. From any angle, through every crevice of tree and rock, the views are breathtaking.

Amy climbs stiffly out of the minibus.

Her legs shake, her lips feel cracked and dry. She hovers awkwardly at the edge of the group. Caught in its cosy bonding, it seems unaware of her.

With a gasp of delight she absorbs her surroundings. To her left, stone walls are banked by deep-green cypresses, which point like giant fingers towards the great clear dome of sky. On her right, tiered gardens, shot with the brilliance of pink roses and orange geraniums, dip from stone terraces and fall, clinging, to the hillside, miraculously at one with it.

Ahead of her the villa beckons, its façade bleached a pale yellow under the glare of the sun. On its wide sweep of porch, massive terracotta pots spill lavender-blue hydrangeas in extravagant disarray. They have been recently watered: shallow pools glitter on the tiled floor, the blooms wink in refreshment.

A man appears at the centre of the arched doorway, lighting its darkness. He wears white trousers and, gently looped into them, an exquisite open-necked silk shirt, the colour of the midday sky. His straight jet-black hair is carefully combed on to his forehead, his face is neat, his body slender and compact.

His hands gesture in welcome. "Ladies and gentlemen, *buon giorno*."

His voice is soft, lilting.

"My name is Marcello Galanti."

I've found him!

A thrill of relief surges through Amy's heart. The relief turns to sour indignation and resentful anger — he is so alive, so normal, living through the routines of his life, while Mum lies cold and buried — then back again to a light-headed triumph at her own determination and success.

She forces herself to listen to what Marcello is saying.

"Welcome to my villa . . . *Per favore* . . . I ask you to walk into the shade for a few moments to recover from the heat of your journey."

The group murmurs appreciation. It moves towards him on to the porch. Amy lingers. She stands at the back, her head down, behind a tall American in a garish checked jacket that hangs from his broad shoulders like a weary tablecloth.

"The Villa Galanti," Marcello launches into what is obviously his much-practised introduction, "was originally a monastery, built, we believe, in the fourteenth century or even earlier. It has been restored and rebuilt several times. During the Second World War it was again damaged. Afterwards, my family bought it and once more attended to many restorations."

He flashes an easy smile at the group.

"Twelve years ago, my father, he die, and the villa became my most treasured inheritance. I decide to renovate the interior completely and to begin work on all my surrounding land.

"Before I took control, a thousand olive trees, they flourish here. Now, as you will see, I have created – sure, every day I continue to create – the most beautiful hanging gardens."

Amy grits her teeth. She takes off her sunglasses and

pushes them into her bag, steeling her eyes against the sun's glare. Beads of sweat slither down her back.

"The gardens," Marcello continues blithely, "although they are planned with great care and precision, I want them always to look natural, wild almost, absolutely without formal lines. They are intended to blend seamlessly with the magnificent hill of Fiesole."

Amy steps back, away from the group and to its left-hand side, so that Marcello can see her clearly. She pulls off her sunhat. Her hair falls, thick, ruffled, on to her shoulders. In the sunlight it glows a fiery copper.

She looks directly into Marcello's face.

Their eyes meet. His are the blue-green of a peacock's tail. A rainbow of recognition flashes between them and hangs suspended in the radiant air.

Marcello's olive skin pales.

"To blend with the hill of Fiesole," he repeats falteringly, as if reciting a prayer.

He steps back, pulls from his pocket a dazzling white handkerchief. He holds the linen to his mouth and with it the scent of Blue Grass, as if the perfume alone gives his lungs freedom to breathe.

Amy flinches at the scent. It is the one her mother always wore.

Marcello's eyes never leave her face.

There is a moment of absolute silence. The group waits, curious, watchful. On the hillside, every leaf is still.

Marcello flutters the handkerchief across his forehead. His fringe, which a minute ago lay flat and burnished, stands upright in startled spikes. He looks away from Amy and scans the faces of the group.

"*Scusi*, ladies and gentlemen. I am very sorry. I feel suddenly most unwell."

He turns and beckons to a figure standing in the shadows of the hall. He mutters a few quiet words to her. She nods and moves towards him.

"My secretary, Claudia —" Marcello's voice sounds thick as clotted cream — "she will take care of you . . . *Mi dispiace* . . . "

He swings away. He walks with quick, agitated strides, through an archway, stuffing the handkerchief back into his pocket. A heavy wooden door closes behind him.

The group sighs.

Without his presence, the hall is immediately a darker place.

Amy stands on the topmost terrace. One hand clutches her hat and bag, the other the burning stone of the balcony. The sun beats on to her bare neck like a drum.

The group flap and twitter beneath her, in among the gardens with Claudia, exclaiming their enchantment. Wisps of voices, fragments of words, float upward and evaporate. Far below — it is as if Amy stands on top of the world — the terracotta roofs and yellow walls of Florence sprawl like pebbles on an enormous beach. The Duomo bulges its benign hat above it, a calm and watchful lighthouse.

A bird pipes insistently into the still air: "Have you *been* to Ur*bi*no, Ur*bi*no?"

I'm going to stand here, exactly where I am, looking at that valley, until Marcello comes out to me. I'm not getting back in that minibus for love or money.

The minutes throb silently away.

If I get any hotter, I shall dissolve. All he will find of me will be a dress and a hat.

Out of nowhere a few huge globs of rain begin to fall. Amy stares in disbelief at the dark polka dots on the balcony, the shiny beads of moisture on her arms. She tips her face at the sky, feeling on her cheeks a few scattered drops. They dry almost immediately and stop. The leaves on the trees bend and rustle, then they burn again in stillness.

Where is he? What's he doing? He knows I'm here. Why doesn't he come?

She hears a faint rustle behind her. It gets louder. Footsteps crunch across the path, slowly at first. Then they come closer, moving to a faster beat. They do not quite break into a run.

Amy's heart clenches in fright. She dares not look round.

If he killed my mother, perhaps he'll kill me too. Trap me in the villa, throw my body down the hillside. I shouldn't be here. Jules warned me. I'm playing with fire.

She tries to straighten her trembling knees, clutching the warmth of the balcony more firmly than it has ever been held before.

Directly behind her, the footsteps stop.

"Tell me I am not mistaken." The voice falters and chokes. "That I am not in a dream. You are Lauren's daughter?"

A hand brushes her arm, grasps her shoulder, swings her round to face him.

"You are the *image* of your mother."

He backs away, his eyes glittering with pain.

"You can only be Amy Grant."

Amy nods, pressing her lips together. If she tries to speak, she knows the tears behind her eyes will spurt in floods and drown the words away.

"Your father, does he know you are here?"

Amy shakes her head.

"And your brother?"

Amy finds her voice. "No." She wills herself to steady it. "Nobody else knows."

"But your brother, he tell you where I am?"

"Julian refused to tell me anything about you."

"Then . . . " Marcello looks bewildered. "How you find me?"

Amy fumbles in her bag, pulls out of it the battered postcard. Wordlessly, she pushes it into Marcello's hands.

"Dio!" His fingers tremble, smooth their tips over it. "Your mother gave you this?"

"Of course not."

"Then how?"

"I found it." Amy's answers come in staccato bursts. "By accident. On the floor."

"When?"

"A few weeks ago."

Is that all it was? I feel as if I've had that card all my life.

She runs a hand through her hair. It is burning hot. "Before then, I hadn't heard of you."

"So Lauren . . . "

"She never spoke of you."

"Ah." Sharply, he turns his head away, as if she had stabbed him in the neck. The card falls to his side. "I hoped she'd have told you."

"Told me what?"

The blue-green eyes meet hers. "She was planning to live with me."

"*What?*"

"And to bring you with her. She said she would only come if you came too."

"To live here? At the Villa Galanti?"

"Where else?"

"I don't believe you." Tiny pinpricks of diamond light begin to sparkle in the shadows closing around her.

"Ah, Amy. It is the truth. Your mother . . . "

"I thought you killed her!"

He spreads his arms in a gesture both passionate and pathetic. "She was the love of my life."

The sunlight has completely disappeared. Amy's legs give way to the darkness. Marcello springs towards her. The scent of Blue Grass fills her head.

He catches her before she falls.

She hears him say, "*Che succede?* It is the heat. Come, lean on me. Let me take you indoors."

12

Afterwards, Amy could not remember crossing the garden, only that the cool shade of the hall came as an immediate and welcome relief.

As they walked through the loggia, she became aware of Marcello's arm around her waist, the taut muscles of his back. He was shorter than Dad, a smaller man, and younger; perhaps even ten years younger. Younger than Mum.

The loggia opened on to a long terrace whose high arched windows overlooked the valley. A table had been laid for coffee. Marcello made her sit. She dipped her head between her knees, trying to get the world into proper focus.

Marcello vanished. He came back a minute later with two elegant curved glasses. "Here, drink this."

The brandy stung her throat. She coughed. He swallowed his in one easy, practised gulp. He stood over her, watching while she emptied her glass. Then he poured the coffee, added brown sugar, stirred, and handed her a cup.

"Thank you." It was an effort to speak.

He sat beside her, near enough for her to notice the dark hair covering the backs of his hands, his manicured fingernails, the immaculate crease in his white trousers. The dark aroma of coffee rose into the air.

Marcello's blue-green eyes locked into hers. "We have much to say to each other."

She nodded. The hot liquid gave her strength, cleared her vision of the diamond sparks dancing across the floor.

"Will you have lunch with me? Spend the afternoon here, so we can talk?"

"Yes."

"Amy, Amy." He ran his hands through his hair. "I did not kill your mother. I do not know what happened that morning. I was not there. Please, you must believe it."

Amy forced the question out of her mouth. The words emerged slowly, as if they walked towards Marcello in a funeral procession. "Are you telling me the truth?"

Marcello reached out for her hand, his fingers amazingly cool. He lifted her hand to his lips but they did not touch it. She wanted them to. She wanted, more than anything, the reassurance, the touch, of his mouth. His eyes flickered at her, making her heart lurch.

"Only the truth," he said.

"Everything began six years ago, on 14th April."

He leaned against the stone balcony, facing her.

"I was flying to London that afternoon for a sale at Christie's. Claudia and I quickly checked the post. There was a letter from Lauren Grant. She'd seen a feature on my gardens in a magazine, asked whether I would grant her permission to use the photographs, how much they would cost.

"I told Claudia to ring her and suggest we meet at my hotel in London the following afternoon." He gave Amy a wry smile. "For your English afternoon tea. I said I would bring with me some more recent photos. When I reached Browns Hotel, there was a message saying she would meet me. I thought no more about her.

"Next morning, I went to Christie's. I bought nothing. I had lunch alone. It was badly cooked. It was raining. The traffic was a nightmare, there were no taxis. I was tired, soaked to the skin. All I wanted was a hot bath and to be on my plane home.

"Lauren was waiting for me in the lounge, in one of the armchairs by the window." Marcello turned away to gaze out at the valley. His hands clenched by his sides, his voice softened. "I shall never forget that moment. I thought: Good God, she is the one I have been looking for."

Amy was astonished at the surge of jealousy that enveloped her. Lucky Mum! To have Marcello fall headlong in love with her, just by sitting in an armchair!

Marcello looked round at Amy with a fleeting smile. "I gave nothing away. We smiled politely, I ordered tea. I took out the photos I had grabbed from my office. I discovered to my dismay they were the wrong ones, taken of very early work on the gardens. They were useless for Lauren's purposes.

"I apologised. Lauren was charming. She wanted to see the early photos. She said the project would make a marvellous book. We began to talk about the Villa Galanti. I told her of its history."

Your famous "introduction". Mum must have been spellbound, gazing into your eyes. Imagining this valley, this villa . . .

Marcello sat, staring into space, locked in his memories. He went on talking, but Amy only half listened. What did the details matter now? All the explanations in the world weren't going to bring Mum back.

Amy and Marcello ate lunch on the terrace. At first she did not think she could swallow anything. But the food was light and succulent: gentle, slippery pasta; pink rack of lamb with aubergines; pungent, grainy cheese.

Marcello told Amy how Lauren and Julian had paid him a surprise visit at the villa that August. Marcello had persuaded them to spend the rest of their stay with him.

How he and Lauren had walked and talked. They had planned a book about the Villa Galanti they would write together, during the autumn and into the winter months.

"We kept it secret, that we were writing a book together. I had all the photographs. I could tell Lauren how I had restored the villa and created the gardens from a thousand olive trees. She put it all into better English than mine." The blue-green eyes smiled at her. "Much better."

Amy said awkwardly, "But your English is excellent."

He brushed aside the compliment. "I wrote this card," he stroked it with his thumb, "the afternoon she left with Julian. I took them to the airport. Then I drove into Florence and paced the streets trying to find her a gift: something to show her she had captured my heart. Scarves, perfume, pottery – they all seemed so ridiculous. So I bought this haunting image and spelt out what I felt.

"It was the only written message I ever sent her. We had to be careful. I telephoned her at times we had arranged. She wrote to me: long, wonderful letters. I still read them. I shall keep them always."

"After she left, where did you meet?"

A cloud of sadness had settled over Amy. Talking about Mum in ways she never had before – as if she were a stranger from a long-distant past – stabbed her with pain.

"I came often to London. From the moment she arrived at the villa we were deeply in love. I saw it in her eyes. She saw it in mine."

"And Julian?"

Where on earth was my poor brother in all this?

"He did not like me. He was jealous. He noticed his mother's happiness. Children are quick to see such things."

Amy thought of Dad and Hannah. "They sure are."

Marcello, deeply meshed in his own story, did not notice her bitterness.

"When did you decide to live together?"

The enormity of her question struck her afresh. She could not believe she might have spent the last six years of her life here, separated from Dad, Jules, Ruth, high in this villa, among these gardens. She'd never have met Chris.

"In early December. Our book was complete. I had closed the villa to the public. Alone here, with only the staff – we were restoring some bedrooms – I pined for Lauren. Each time we met, it became harder to say goodbye."

"But she was *married!*" A wave of anger flooded through her.

"I know. She loved your father, Amy. For her, it was a most difficult decision. She had to leave her family, her English life, everything."

"And you think she'd have done that for *you?*"

"She had the date set for the middle of January, when the villa would be finished." He looked at her. "One suite was specially planned for you."

Amy flushed, outraged. So much had happened without her having an inkling. To hide her anger, she asked, "How did you find out . . . ?"

"About the accident?" Marcello clasped his hands until the skin turned white. "I rang Lauren one morning in Grayshott, as we had arranged. There was no answer. I had a black feeling in my heart. I caught the first plane to London. At Browns, I rang her again. Another woman answered. I asked if I could speak to Lauren. The woman said, 'No,' and the line went dead. I spent a sleepless night.

"Next morning I hired a car. I drove to Grayshott in the snow. The traffic was terrible. I was frantic. I reached your village around midday. I bought a newspaper. The head-lines . . . " His voice trailed away. "I sat in the pub, listening to the gossip.

"I wanted to see you, talk to you, although I knew you couldn't . . . I drove past your house, parked a few houses away. I felt – how you say? – numb. As if someone had chopped out my heart and thrown it into the snow. I wished they had. In that car, then, I also wanted to die."

"How long did you stay in Grayshott?"

"I drove back to London that night." He spread his hands. "I was powerless, useless. I could do nothing . . . Except grieve."

When it grows cooler and the last group leave, Amy and Marcello walk in the gardens. He takes her down the hillside, shows her the spectacular views, the trees, the glory of roses and geraniums, the places they will plant in the autumn.

He falls silent, silhouetted against the Florentine valley. Shadows have deepened beneath his eyes. "You haven't asked me one important question."

"You've told me so much."

"*Certo*. I have wanted to meet you for so long. But think, Amy. What drew your mother and I so quickly together?"

Amy frowns. "The villa? Your photos? . . . Of course, your book."

"Exactly. You haven't asked me where it is."

"It was *published*?"

"I only wish . . . " He presses his lips together. "But if you like, I can show you where it is. Your own private view . . . One nobody else has seen."

*

They walk up the steep luxuriant slopes towards the villa, then beyond the porch to the left-hand side of the house, where a narrow pebbly path winds into the hills.

They start to climb. To their left, cypresses herald the edge of the forest. Its density of trees towers over them, casting monumental shadows.

I wouldn't want to spend the night alone in there!

Amy watches Marcello stride ahead of her, intent, purposeful, suddenly reminded how she had watched Dad that dawn, jogging through the garden.

Marcello swerves to the left. A narrow, half-hidden flight of steps struggles into the trees. He scrambles up, brushing aside the overhanging branches for Amy to pass. The forest clears on to a brief plateau.

A small chapel hunches in front of them. Its stone walls, faded pink and yellow, are battered by wind and rain, burned by the sun. Ivy clambers between the stones, along the narrow windows, caking the dome of roof. A splintering wooden door, beaten by time, closes a weary mouth against them.

Marcello fumbles for a key. He swings open the door and beckons.

Amy steps inside. The cool, damp air lingers over her skin, making her shiver. The floor, rough, unkempt, bulges unevenly beneath her feet; the walls crumble apologetically behind matted cobwebs. The roof looks as if it will fall on her shoulders if she so much as raises her voice. She can smell mice and wild garlic – and the darker, insidious odour of neglect.

A wooden chest stands in the centre of the chapel, like a shrine. On it perches a candlestick. Its slim, white candle has never been lit.

Marcello stands against the furthest wall.

"This little chapel was built by Franciscan monks in the seventeenth century. And on this wall –" he sweeps his arm up to it – "the experts tell us, is a fresco of *Christ's Last Supper* by Nicodemo Ferruci."

Amy stares up at it, at the mass of dingy, swirling colours, patchy fragments of paint. She can make out the heads and shoulders of men at a long table, and the central figure of Christ, but their faces, the vital details, are lost. Flashes of paint – gold and aquamarine – wink among the Apostles like dragonflies in amber.

"In the chest," Marcello gestures towards it, "lie the manuscript and photos of our book. When your mother died, I hid them there. Umberto and I, together we carry the chest from my villa to this *cappellina*."

Amy looks down at it. She remembers standing in the

Surrey graveyard in the biting wind, clutching Dad's hand. Now it feels as if Mum lies buried here, high on this hill, hidden in the beauty of this crumbling sacred space.

"If Lauren had lived and the book had been published, we would have spent the money on restoring this chapel and the fresco. I had a contract with a publisher in Rome . . . I cancelled it . . . My *cappellina* will stay like this until it crumbles entirely into dust and the wind blows it away."

Later, they stand looking at each other on the villa's porch.

"Tonight, I have an engagement," Marcello says. "*Mi dispiace*. Umberto will drive you back to your hotel in my car." He flicks his handkerchief across his forehead. "You leave for Grayshott on Saturday?"

Amy nods.

In less than forty-eight hours, I'll be home.

"Tomorrow . . . " Marcello's eyes search her face. "You have a free day, no? You will come again here?" His voice drops. "You will read our book?"

Amy hesitates. The thought of another lonely day in Florence fills her with dread. She longs to open the chest, to touch the book — to hold a part of Mum in her hands. And she wants to see Marcello.

He reads her thoughts. "I will take only yes for an answer.

Umberto, he will pick you up from your hotel at ten o'clock."

"Thank you."

"*Prego*. And Amy . . . " Marcello looks thinner, haunted. "May I keep the postcard?"

She feels blood rising to her face. "Of course. It belongs to you."

Marcello gives a little formal bow. "Until tomorrow, then."

"Yes. Until tomorrow."

13

Amy slithered out of the Mercedes, thanked Umberto and walked up to her room.

It puffed a stifling heat.

She perched on the bed, trembling with exhaustion and, unexpectedly, on the verge of tears. She refused to let herself cry.

Mission accomplished, she told herself sternly. *I've achieved what I came here to do. I should be celebrating.*

She kicked off her sandals. The pillows felt warm and dusty beneath her head.

The morning's anticipation, the heady feelings of achievement and success, had dwindled to disappointment. Talking about Mum had stirred the old pain into a potent, fresh brew. She realised how little she'd known about Mum's life – and that she'd opened a Pandora's box of secrets. What might come exploding out of it?

Could she really trust Marcello? He was so handsome, so seductive. If he wasn't Mum's killer, who was? Had she come searching in quite the wrong place? Could the culprit – assuming there was one – be much closer to home? What other clues might there be, maybe right under her nose in Grayshott, that could have led her, long ago, to the truth?

Amy stripped off her clothes and stepped into the shower. She shut her eyes, letting the cool water stream over her body.

The answer to everything is in my head. In that memory of mine that won't unlock itself, however hard I try.

She wrapped herself in a towel, flung open the window and stood on the balcony. The sky had lost its radiance. Surly banks of cloud swirled up from the horizon, yet the heat had not abated. Perhaps those drops of rain on the terrace were the prelude to a storm?

I haven't solved anything. I've scraped at the surface of the truth. I'm terrified of what I'm going to find. But I'm not giving up.

The sounds of early evening drifted towards her: children bickering; a baby crying; a woman's voice singing a lullaby. Tinkling scales plodded up and down a piano. A dog barked. Amy longed to be home.

Perhaps if I stop trying so hard to remember that ghastly morning, stop being so furious that I've blanked it out, it'll come back to me. Just like I found my voice again, from out of nowhere.

She pulled on a clean pair of jeans and a pale pink cotton shirt. Not a breath of air stirred in the room.

I need to walk. Into the city, anywhere. Out of this furnace. It's got to be cooler outside.

Amy slips out to the Via Guiccardini, over the Ponte Vecchio, past the Uffizi and into the Piazza della Signoria. Crowds sit on the street steps or at café tables. The square buzzes with voices, the chink of cutlery on china, the clink of glasses on tabletops.

She walks towards the Café Rivoire. It sprawls elegantly on a corner, framed by low iron railings and interwoven terracotta pots bright with geraniums and laurel.

She decides to have a fruit juice and a sandwich at the Rivoire before going back to her room. She scans the crowd of drinkers, trying to find a space.

Two pairs of eyes look up at her from a nearby table.

They belong to Julian and Christopher.

Amy gasps. Their faces are tanned, relaxed, unshaven; their hair longer. They wear white shirts rolled to their elbows. Startled, they stare back at her as if they cannot believe their eyes.

There is no escape for her, no hiding place.

She longs to walk into Chris's arms, explain why she ran away, tell him how she feels. But Julian's presence makes her freeze. She can only stand there looking like a naughty child.

"Amy?" Julian scrambles to his feet. "What the *hell* are you doing here?"

Amy tries to smile, to pretend she often spends her time walking around Florence. Chris meets her eyes. He flushes, first with what looks like relief and delight, then with embarrassment. He says nothing, glances quickly away.

"Hi, Jules," Amy says bleakly. She plays for time. "I could ask you the same!"

"We've been here all week. We drove here from Perugia. I wanted to show Chris the city before we go to Rome."

He stands nearer to her now, by the café's border. He smells faintly of sweat and sun. He lowers his voice. "What are you doing here? Who are you with?"

"I'm on my own." Amy looks over Julian's shoulder, trying to see Chris.

"*Why* are you here?"

"Why d'you think?"

"I thought you were in Paris."

"I decided there was something more important I had to do."

Julian's eyes narrow. "Would Marcello have anything to do with it?"

"Of course he would." She spits out the words with a passion that surprises her.

Julian is beginning to understand. "I thought you'd destroyed that postcard. I told you to forget about him."

"I'm not a little girl any more, Jules. I don't always do what my bossy older brother tells me."

"So I see." Julian looks taken aback.

"If you'd *told* me about Marcello, I wouldn't have had to come here to find him."

"So your being here is *my* fault?"

"I didn't say that . . . I'm old enough to be responsible for my own actions."

"Hmm . . . " Julian doesn't sound convinced. "And *have* you found him?"

"As a matter of fact I have."

"*When* did you –"

"Today . . . at his villa." Amy flings her hair back defiantly. "We spent the day together. He asked me to lunch."

"I *bet* he did!"

"And he's invited me back tomorrow."

Julian leans one hand on the railing and leaps over it. He grabs Amy's arm. "Oh, no, he hasn't!"

"His driver's picking me up. You can't stop me going."

"Yes, I bloody well can." Julian's voice shakes with rage. "Does Dad know you're here?"

"Of course not. He thinks I'm in Paris."

"If you see Marcello again, I'll tell Dad what you've been up to."

Amy catches her breath. "You wouldn't *do* that."

"Just you watch me." Julian grabs Amy's shoulders. "I don't want you to have anything to do with Marcello. He's dangerous."

"Rubbish." Amy pulls away. "Anyway, it's too late. We talked for hours. He loved Mum."

"He'd no *right* to, sis. She was married. He should never have –"

"What? What *did* he do?"

Julian's arms drop to his sides. "I don't know." Beads of sweat glitter on his forehead. "I was only thirteen. Mum never told me."

Amy senses she has the upper hand. "I *do* know, because I've taken the trouble to find out. Marcello –"

"That's enough!" Julian lays a finger over her mouth. "I don't want to know. I don't *ever* want to hear his name again."

Amy steps back from her brother, filled with contempt. "Coward." She turns her back on him, flounces away. "I'm going back to my hotel."

But she's frightened he'll abandon her.

Julian catches up. "Sorry, sis, I didn't mean to bully you . . . When are you leaving Florence?"

Half reluctantly, she says, "Saturday."

"At least we've found each other. Come and have a drink. A meal. Let's talk about tomorrow."

Amy looks back at him and then at Chris. She takes a deep breath. "OK. But only because I'm dying of thirst."

Julian muttered, "Sorry, Chris. Family argument. Sorted."

Chris said, "Hi, Amy," but hardly looked at her. She drank an orange juice, listening to Julian's account of Perugia; his praise of Florence's magnificent art. It began to rumble with rain.

They had supper at a nearby restaurant. Miserably, Amy wondered how she was going to turn Marcello's invitation down. If she didn't, she knew Julian would carry out his threat.

As they left, Julian said, "I'll walk you to your hotel. We need to talk. Chris, see you back at ours."

"Good night, Amy." Chris looked directly at her, a spark of intimacy in his brief smile.

Amy's heart leapt.

Julian took her arm as they stepped on to the wet cobblestones. "Write Marcello a note. Tell him you can't come tomorrow."

The temperature in the streets had dropped dramatically. Amy shivered. "But I've already said yes."

"Make an excuse." Julian held his umbrella over her. Rain thundered on to it like bullets from a gun. "I'm only trying to protect you."

"It'll sound so rude."

"You made the effort to find him. He can hardly complain. Leave the note for the driver with the concierge. Be sensible, sis, and I promise I won't tell Dad."

"And tomorrow?"

"Spend the day with Chris and me. We're going to Siena. It's the most beautiful little place in the world."

Dear Marcello

I'm very sorry but I can't come to your villa today. Julian is in Florence. I bumped into him last night. I'd no idea he was here.

He's forbidden me to see you again. He's still very angry about what happened between you and Mum. He's threatened to tell Dad I came to Florence to find you unless I do what he says.

Thank you for talking to me, and for showing me all you did.

Amy Grant

She labelled the envelope — *Umberto. Please give this to Marcello Galanti* — gave it to the concierge and explained who it was for. Then, before she changed her mind, she forced herself to leave the hotel.

Julian drove the small hired Fiat, Chris sat next to him.

Amy tried not to stare at Chris's neck, the curl of his ears, his arm, tanned, gleaming with blond hair, as he flung it along the seat. He did not turn to look at her.

They drove out of Florence, on to the *autostrada*, through the hillside tunnels, past the American Memorial, into the landscape of Tuscany, filled with umbrella pine and bright fields of triumphant sunflowers.

Julian described *Il Palio*, the festival of Siena. "It happens every year on 16th August. That was yesterday." He grinned at Chris. "Sorry, we're a day late! It's a race between lots of *contrade*. They ride magnificent horses and wear amazing costumes. It's all over in a few minutes, but the passion they put into it!"

Amy wondered bitterly whether she'd ever have a chance to talk to Chris without Julian at their elbow. She had to tell Chris how she felt about him. And she was fast running out of time.

They sit in the Piazza del Campo, drinking thick sweet coffee at the Bar il Palio.

Amy is so close to Chris their shoulders almost brush. Julian talks endlessly about the beauty of the square.

Amy interrupts. "I'm going to buy a book on Siena. I'd like something to take home, to remind me."

Julian waves an arm impatiently. "Over there, sis. On that stall. Make sure it's in English!"

Amy walks towards it. She is suddenly aware that someone is watching her: a middle-aged man dressed in bottle-green trousers and a matching shirt. His face is swarthy, pockmarked. A bright red beret perches rakishly on his oily hair.

Amy feels his laser-beam eyes on her. Trying to ignore him, she heads for the stall, opens her bag to find her purse. The man has moved closer. Far too close. She can smell his garlic breath.

He hisses like a snake into her face. He whips out of his pocket something pale. It has teeth. It is a dirty ivory comb. Before Amy can move, he has drawn the comb down the side of her hair in a swift, raking movement, pulling at its roots.

Amy screams. She jumps away from him and drops her bag. In a flash, Julian and Chris are by her side. Julian darts towards the man, shoves at him, starts shouting.

Chris takes her arm and steadies her. "Are you hurt?"

Amy shakes her head, but her teeth chatter with shock. "Thanks, Chris . . . I'm fine."

"Thank God for that!"

He stoops with her to pick up the contents of her bag. They scatter on the pavement like a child's toys: a lipstick rolling in its shiny case, loose coins, a felt-tip pen.

Their hands meet over a slim red-leather book and the crushed petals of a faded yellow rose.

14

Amy seizes the moment.

"I didn't mean to run away from you."

Crowds press heedlessly past, almost treading on her hands, knocking against her shoulder. The pavement sways around her. She rescues her bag from under someone's feet, clutching it like a long-lost friend.

Chris kneels beside her, frantically scooping up her passport, her purse, a small plastic-framed mirror. In it, for a split second, she sees his face. She looks sideways at him. Chris bites his lip and looks silently back. Something changes in his eyes and gives her hope.

Make him listen.

Incoherently, the words spill out of her. "That night. There were other people in the garden. I'm so sorry. You must've thought . . . I can explain . . . Please let me."

Chris picks up the sonnets, tenderly brushes the dirt from the soft binding. "It's OK, Amy, you don't have to say anything."

She scrapes up the rose petals, cradling them in her palm. "You've no idea how I feel . . . Please, Chris, can we talk?"

He cuts in decisively. "OK, then." He turns towards her. "Tonight."

He opens the book and holds it out to her.

Amy's lungs catch with relief. She slides the battered rose among the pages. "When? What about Julian? How can we . . . "

Chris mutters, "Leave him to me."

He stands up. "Everything's fine, Jules," he says loudly. "Amy wasn't hurt. We've managed to rescue her things."

"Are you sure, sis?" Julian looks at her anxiously.

"I'm fine. Don't make a fuss."

He gives her an awkward hug. "What a lunatic guy! Thank God he didn't have a knife. It doesn't bear thinking about . . . *Sure* you're OK?"

Amy zips up her bag. *Tonight!* The colours of the square sing to her; the delicate blue sky shimmers with delight; crowds skim across the courtyard, chasing the sun. "Quite sure."

"Excellent. I'm going to buy you that book you wanted. And then, hey, why don't we all have lunch to celebrate? My treat."

Amy looks up at Chris. "Sometimes my brother has really wonderful ideas."

*

They walk Siena's narrow streets, linger in a pottery shop.

Julian buys a hand-painted plate, haggling over the price. Chris catches Amy's eye. They smile at each other like conspirators.

They eat lunch out of doors. Julian disappears to pay the bill. Chris leans across the table and says, "I have a plan!"

Julian hauls them off to the cathedral. They stand looking up at the façade, gasping at its beauty. It towers against the sky like a huge encrusted jewel. Julian waves an arm, moves forward to describe its details. "The lower part of the façade was built by Giovanni Pisano in 1284."

Amy feels Chris's hand, gently and for a single fleeting moment, press against the small of her back.

In Florence, they eat supper in the same restaurant.

Chris toasts Julian over a glass of wine. "You're an excellent driver and a brilliant guide."

Julian replies it is a pleasure to have such a captive and adoring audience. They laugh.

They stand outside, breathing the cool night air; walk towards the river. Lights in the water gleam like fireflies. The sky, showered in handfuls of pin-prick stars, deepens to an inky blue.

Chris says firmly, "It's OK, Jules . . . I'll walk Amy back to her hotel."

Julian looks at Chris. "Fine," he says. "I'll go and pack." He gives Amy a hug. "Will you be OK getting to the airport?"

"Yes, Jules," Amy says patiently.

"See you at Terra Firma in a couple of weeks." He steps away from them and waves. "Night, sis."

For a whole, long heartbeat, Florence is a silent city.

Amy and Chris look at each other. They move closer together. They walk on to the Ponte Vecchio. Chris slides an arm around Amy's waist. He pulls her towards the centre of the bridge, where they can stand and watch the river, undisturbed.

"Talk to me," he says.

Amy tells him about Dad and Hannah in the garden. The postcard in Mum's study. Julian's refusal to tell her anything. Her decision to find Marcello. Lying to Dad and Ruth. Being at the Villa Galanti. Seeing the wooden chest in the chapel. Never wanting to tell Dad what she'd seen.

Chris listens. He turns towards her, smoothes her hair out of her eyes. "You've got to let your dad start again."

Amy looks up at him. "That's what Ruth says, what Julian says. I know you're right. But it's so hard to accept. Nobody can ever take Mum's place."

"Nobody's trying to." Chris slides his arms around her. "Your dad's found Hannah because he knows you're going to set him free."

"I hadn't thought of it like that . . . "

"And you can set him free, because you're not a little girl any longer."

"Sometimes," Amy says, "I feel like a child. I want to burst into tears and be comforted. I want my mum." Her eyes burn. "And other times . . . "

"Yes?"

Something in Amy melts. "I just want to be kissed. But nobody's ever offered. Nobody I ever cared about."

Chris takes his cue. "So can I, finally, kiss you?"

Her heart races. "Yes."

"You won't run away again?"

She laughs. "I promise not to."

He runs a finger down the side of her cheek, over her mouth; draws her body towards his. "That's just as well, Amy. Because this time, I won't let you get away."

On the plane, after it had taken off, Amy opened the letter.

It had been waiting for her with the concierge at the hotel. She knew it was from Marcello: she recognised his handwriting. In the shadowy hallway, then in her room, she couldn't face reading it. Not after such an evening. She sat on the lonely bed, remembering Christopher's kisses; drifted to sleep feeling his lips on hers, hearing the murmur of his voice, telling her he'd write . . .

Now, high within the walls of cloud, she steeled herself. She drew out the thick, creamy notepaper with its sepia crest, its scent of Blue Grass:

Dear Amy

I am greatly sorry you could not come today. All night, I have been thinking about you. But I understand the reason.

Thank you, really, from the bottom of my heart, for coming here to find me. I only want to say now one thing. If you ever wish to see me again, I shall be here waiting. My private number is at the top of the page. Any time, ring me.

I loved your mother. I know you have believed it.

Marcello

Amy stared at the letter with a confusion of feelings: sadness, anger, resignation, profound dissatisfaction.

She'd solved nothing. Perhaps there was nothing to solve. She had no choice but to believe Marcello's story. But so many things in it didn't add up. What about the book? Surely if Marcello had really loved Mum, he'd want to publish it as a memorial to her, not freeze her inheritance under a pile of stone.

Unless it hid his guilt . . .

Amy shivered. Perhaps she could go back to see Marcello and persuade him to publish it. Give him permission – if any were needed – to unlock Mum from her tomb.

Did she have the courage? Would she have to tell Dad the whole story? Would Marcello agree? Was there, after these six long years, a last chapter to be written that Amy could help him with?

She'd come to Italy with a postcard and left it with a letter. Had she really achieved anything?

Of course, she'd found Chris again. She remembered those kisses on the Ponte Vecchio. They'd been worth everything.

Amy opened the front door of Terra Firma.

The house smelt of polish. Fresh roses graced the hall table. A bowl of apples and bananas spilled over in the kitchen, a note beside it. Dora said Tyler was fine and she'd bring him home tomorrow night, when everyone was back.

Wearily, Amy plodded up to her room. She took Marcello's letter out of her bag and hid it in her desk. She went to the window, peered out at the garden. The grass had grown. Rose petals showered the lawn. Leaves on the silver birch had flickered into dusty gold; the fairy lights clung tenaciously to their branches.

She remembered the party: the rustle of her dress, standing in Chris's arms, stumbling back to the house over the damp lawn. It all seemed a long time ago.

A blackbird trilled ecstatically, welcoming her home.

Two figures emerged from the shed at the bottom of the garden. They laughed.

Amy turns and races out of the house.

By the time she reaches the shed, the couple have vanished. The thunder of dance music echoes from the sky. There must have been a party on the Common last night that's still spilling over into the late morning . . .

The shed door swings open on its rusty hinge. Amy steps inside. The scent of musk hangs in the air, mixed with the stink of sweat and dark tobacco. Cigarette papers and crushed butts litter the floor.

The couple had pulled some old sacking from a pile in the corner. It lies flattened by their weight. Amy stares down at it. Maybe they'd made love on it all night long, their bodies naked, entwined, while music blared to the sky. She imagines lying there with Chris; tries to quash the wild beating of her heart.

She stoops to pick up the bedding, to put it back where it belongs. She stops. Something made of wood stands half hidden in a corner of the shed. She's never seen it before.

She moves towards it, curious, gripped by dread. She pulls at the one remaining rotten piece of sacking that drapes over it.

Underneath it, lovingly hand-carved, sits a child's cradle.

Amy's hands fly to her mouth, then to the sides of the tiny bed. It begins to rock beneath her touch, creaking as if with joy that once again it is needed.

Amy's head begins to throb.

Had Mum been *pregnant* when she died? Is *that* the key to the mystery?

Amy pushes at the door to Mum's study.

The room fills with echoes.

Ruth's: *"You put your mum on a bit of a pedestal."*

Dad's: *"She wasn't perfect, Amy. Don't make out she was some kind of saint."*

Marcello's: *"She was the love of my life."*

She slides on to the sofa, grabs the Saint Elizabeth cushion and hugs it, brushing impatiently at her face, which seems to be wet.

"Were you the victim in all this, Mum? Or did you just get what was coming to you, living a double life?"

The room throbs with angry silence.

"You see, I've met your Marcello. Oh, yes! I've been to the Villa Galanti. Bit of a paradise, isn't it? I know about your plans, because he told me.

"But what I don't understand is this."

Amy throws the cushion to one side. She stands up, staring hard into those pale grey-green eyes.

"Why didn't you even *mention* them to me? Or were you just going to push me into a suitcase and take me along for the ride?"

"Are you better?" Ruth drags her into the hall.

"Better than what?"

Ruth looks at her. "You were dying of flu, remember?"

Amy flushes. "Sorry, I'd forgotten."

Ruth frowns. "Are you all right?"

"I'm fine."

On the piano, Ruth's dad thunders away at "Land of Hope and Glory" with extraordinary gusto.

"Could we talk in your room?"

"Course. Come up . . . Ignore the mess."

Amy flops on to Ruth's bed. "There's something I've got to tell you."

"I *thought* there was . . . You can't hide anything from Auntie Ruth!"

"No, this is serious." Amy takes a deep breath. "I wasn't ill . . . I lied."

"What?"

"I had to."

"Why?"

"I had to do something on my own and I couldn't trust anyone or tell them, because if anyone had known what I'd planned they wouldn't have let me go."

Ruth sits beside her. "Amy Grant, would you like to slow down and start again?"

"How was Paris?" Amy asks miserably.

"You first. One word at a time. Very, very slowly . . . "

"Hi!" Dad says.

His smile stretches ear to ear. He gives Amy a sharp, perfunctory hug. He looks tanned and fit and – Amy stares at him as he plonks his suitcase in the hall – different. He shines with happiness. It radiates from him like the morning sun.

"How are you, sweetheart?"

"Fine, thanks."

"How was Paris?"

"It was great." Amy does her best to sound enthusiastic. "We had a really interesting time."

"Hope it improved your French."

"Oh, it *did*."

"How did you spend the week?"

Amy tries to remember what Ruth had told her. "Oh, you know . . . we did everything. We went everywhere. All the usual Paris stuff . . . It was very well organised."

"That's Mrs Baxter for you." Dad picks up the post from the hall table. "She's brilliant at that kind of thing." He puts the letters down. "Look, shall we have a cup of tea? I've got something fantastic to tell you."

Amy follows Dad into the kitchen. He isn't walking, he's kind of hopping like a frog. No, he isn't. He's dancing.

She plugs in the kettle and looks at him. "I can see you had a wonderful time."

Dad sits at the table, then leaps to his feet again. "Oh, Amy, it was fabulous. I've never been to Wales before and the mountains are just superb. We walked and walked, wind and rain and sun, it didn't matter."

"Great." Amy holds her breath. "And?"

Dad throws back his head and laughs. "Clever girl. The biggest 'and' in the world! I asked Hannah to marry me and she said yes!"

Amy gasps. The kitchen begins to sway around her. "*Marry you?*"

"That's right. Isn't it wonderful?"

"But you've only just *met*."

"Well, not exactly, but I hear what you're saying. It *has* happened very fast." Dad looks down at his hands. "It was something you said that got me thinking."

"Oh?" Amy's stomach starts to bubble. She grabs the edge of the table, squeezes it, bites her tongue until she can feel the pain.

"About me acting like a besotted teenager." He grins. "You were right!"

"I was?"

I'm supposed to say congratulations. Aren't I?

"Thing is, when you fall in love, it doesn't really matter *how* old you are. It just happens and suddenly you're in it up to your ears."

And I hope you'll be very happy together?

"After Mum died, I thought there'd never be anyone else again and Hannah, she was engaged to a man called Jack, I never knew that before, but she told me a couple of evenings ago. So for both of us, it's second time round the block, but we're absolutely sure we're doing the right thing."

He pauses for breath.

Amy slithers on to the nearest chair. Her feet are so cold she can hardly feel them. "Congratulations," she says mechanically. "I'm very happy for you both."

"I *knew* you would be." Dad's eyes flash with relief and joy. "You've been so wonderful, all these years. I don't know how I'd have got through them without you."

Amy swallows. Her tongue seems to be stuck to the roof of her mouth. She tries desperately to find something polite to say. "Are you going to have a long engagement?"

It's as if she's talking to a stranger.

Dad shakes his head. "We're going to marry in a Register Office as soon as we can, and then have a short blessing at our church. Something simple and dignified. I know Frances will fit us in. She's such a great vicar and she was marvellous when, Mum . . . "

"I see."

"And Hannah says —" Dad's face breaks into the widest smile the world has ever seen — "my darling Hannah says, 'Would you be maid of honour?'"

Amy lurches towards the kitchen sink and heaves into it.

15

"I *knew* it would happen!" Amy paced up and down Ruth's bedroom, hopping over the litter of clothes. "I saw it coming the minute I saw that woman. I could've written the bloody script if they'd asked me!"

"Sit down, Amy. It's like watching a tennis match!"

"But nobody ever does ask me. They go right ahead and do whatever they want. I'm tacked on the end of their plans like a donkey's tail. Splitting up your family and going to live in Italy? Take Amy along for the ride. Getting married again? Let's ask Amy to be maid of honour . . . "

"So what did you *say*?"

"I didn't get a chance to say *anything*. The minute Dad had told me, Dora came banging on the door. Tyler hurtled through it like the soppiest dog in the universe and there was me puking into the sink. Dad told Dora his news —"

"You're wearing the carpet to shreds!"

"And then told Dora I'd *agreed*. God, it's *unbelievable*. Don't I have *any* say?"

"You can hardly refuse, can you? It's not as if Hannah's a

chain-smoking alcoholic nutter about to gobble up her fourth husband."

"But that's exactly it. She's got it all, hasn't she? She's clever and young and beautiful . . . And to crown it all, she's got my dad!"

"Look, if you don't sit down *now*, I'll open the window and you can chuck yourself out of it."

Amy stopped in her tracks. "What? . . . Oh, all right. Shove over."

There was a moment's silence. Ruth seized her opportunity.

"If you saw it coming, it's hardly a surprise."

"But the *speed!*"

"Maybe they've got their reasons. Marrying Hannah's got to be better than skulking out of bedrooms in the middle of the night." Ruth glanced at Amy's flushed cheeks. "There's gossip in the village."

"*I* haven't heard anything."

"It's twitchy net-curtain stuff . . . Mum told me."

"What are they saying?"

"Tut, tut! Two doctors, same practice, is it ethical? Total garbage. But everyone *saw* them together at your party. They obviously meant to make it public."

"You don't understand." Amy clenched her arms round

her body, rocked backwards and forwards. "Hannah will be moving *in*. Into our house . . . *my* house."

"Where else?"

"Last night, she came for supper. She'd unpacked, had a shower, all frightfully efficient. There she was, sitting in Mum's chair, reeking of lily-of-the-valley, looking like the cat who's drunk a barrel of cream."

"She has just got engaged!"

"And there's me like the biggest gooseberry . . . She's spent a whole week with Dad. I haven't seen him for ages. I don't get a chance to talk to him for more than three minutes."

"You got away with your week in Florence without him finding out. You should be *pleased* his attention's elsewhere."

Amy shifted uncomfortably. "Yeah. It sure is that, I can tell you."

"And yours should be too. We've got exam results on Thursday. And a new term soon." Ruth stood up, stretched her long arms above her head. "Forget your dad and Hannah. Let them get married. Look stunning and be a good little maid of honour."

"It's all right for you!"

"Don't forget there'll be other people at the wedding you really want to see." Ruth grinned down at Amy's miserable face. "That brother of yours will be coming back from Rome with a certain special someone in tow."

Amy sniffed. "Yeah, maybe . . . "

"No maybe about it. And he'll be there for *you*."

Amy and Ruth stood in the school crush, opening their envelopes.

"I got straight As," Amy said. The letters jumped up and down in front of her eyes.

Ruth gave her a bear hug. "I got three As, three Bs and two Cs. Thank God you don't have to be a rocket scientist to play the violin."

Amy shoved the envelope into her skirt pocket, feeling relieved but hardly full of joy. "Dad'll be pleased."

"Course, he will, Amy. He'll be *thrilled*."

"I suppose. *If* I can get a word in edgeways."

"How d'you mean?"

"Ever had wedding plans shoved down your throat morning, noon and night?"

"Can't say I have. I thought it was going to be a small family thing?"

"That was bad enough. But it's grown. It's getting totally out of hand."

"Have you heard from Chris?"

"Not yet. Dad caught me waiting for the postman this morning. Asked what I was doing."

Ruth flung an arm around Amy's shoulders. "Eddie and me and some of the gang . . . we're driving into Guildford tonight to celebrate our results."

Amy wasn't listening. "I've read those sonnets so often I know them all by heart."

"Why don't you come with us? Bit of clubbing might cheer you up."

"What, tonight?"

"Come over to mine at eight-thirty. Wear that red dress again. You look gorgeous in it."

Amy stood on one leg, held on to Ruth's shoulder, shook a stone out of her trainer.

"You know what? That's the best offer I've had all week."

"Hi, sweetheart!" Dad pokes his nose round the kitchen door. "That smells wonderful."

He vanishes.

I'm not going to mention my results. I'll just wait and see whether he remembers.

She carries two plates of pasta into the dining room and dumps them on the table. "Supper's ready."

"Brilliant!" Dad stops hovering in the hall. He jumps

about in the doorway, his hands behind his back. "How was your day?"

"Fine."

"Great." Pause. "Do you want to see something very special?"

Amy blushes with pleasure. "Sure."

Perhaps he's remembered and bought me a present. Tickets for something . . . A West End show . . . A weekend in London as a treat for his brilliant daughter.

Dad's hands reappear from behind his back. One of them is holding a small black velvet box. He holds it out to her. "Take a look at this."

Amy gasps. "Is it for me?"

Dad looks sheepish. "Not exactly, sweetheart . . . It's for Hannah."

Amy opens the box. The sapphire winks up at her, crystal cool, sophisticated, nestling in a circle of perfect diamonds.

"It's her engagement —"

Amy grits her teeth. "I can *see* what it is."

"Don't you think it's beautiful?"

"Stunning."

The box snaps its teeth at her fingers. She gives it back to Dad.

"You're not just saying that?"

"No, it's really lovely. Congrat–" The room begins to spin like a child's top.

"Amy? Are you OK?"

"I'm fine . . . Sorry . . . Got something in my eye."

At the bottom of the stairs, she turns. "I'm not all that hungry. I'm going out with Ruth tonight . . . It's getting a bit late, so I'd better go and change."

Amy ran up the stairs two at a time before Dad could follow.

As she reached the landing, the phone rang. She froze. It might be Julian. It might even be Chris. Before she could decide what to do, Dad had answered.

Amy crouched at the top of the stairs, motionless. She held tight to the slippery wood of the banister. A blob of tomato sauce had stained her jeans. It looked like blood and smelt almost as bad.

"Frances? How kind of you to . . . No, it was sweet of you to see Hannah and me this morning. I know how busy you . . . You have? . . . That's *wonderful* . . . Saturday 8th September at noon . . . Perfect . . . It's engraved on my heart . . . Hannah will be thrilled. I'll tell her tonight . . . You're a star, Frances . . . Thank you so much."

Click. Pause. Dad jabbed at the phone.

"Good evening. I wonder if I could speak to Julian Grant?

. . . *Julian* . . . Is he? . . . Could I leave a message? . . . Could
you ask him to telephone his father as soon as possible? . . .
No, it's not bad news . . . It's the best . . . But it's most
important I speak to him tonight . . . Tell him to ring me any
time, it doesn't matter how late . . . Thank you . . . Good
night."

Amy released the banister. She dashed into the bathroom
and locked the door. She turned on the radio and all the taps,
full blast.

In Guildford, the Wizard throbs with noise. It thunders out
into the street, which rocks with the sound.

Ruth and Eddie and the gang, dragging Amy with them,
have slunk quickly through the door saying they are all
"eighteen, going on nineteen". Amy feels ninety-eight. The
doorman is dealing with a drunk and hardly notices.

Someone hands her a tall glass of something cold. Fresh
and potent, like cider. Amy drinks it fast, to give her
confidence.

Someone else asks her to dance. In the crush of bodies it's
almost impossible to move. Her partner has a Mohican
haircut. He's dyed the crest a bright pink to match his shirt,
which flops undone to his waist. He has wide, coal-black,
spaced-out eyes.

After a while he disappears into the crowd and Amy cannot see him.

She dances on her own.

The beat of the music thunders in her ears. The strobe lights flash around her, turning her red dress into an inky black, a lime green, a luminous orange. Her hair tumbles to her shoulders.

When the track ends, someone else pushes another drink into her hands. This one has a great kick. It tastes like honey and orange and aniseed and gin and caffeine rolled into one glorious sickly combination.

It slides, thick and fiery, down her throat.

She shoots on to the dance floor again, by herself. This time it doesn't seem so crowded. In fact, it seems as if nobody else is dancing, only her. Though lots of people are watching. Their eyes, when she happens to glimpse them, wink at her under the lights like that sapphire in its bed of diamonds.

She kicks off her shoes and dances on. Her dress slips from one shoulder but it doesn't matter. It simply gives her more freedom to move. Much more . . .

She flings out her arms, twirls this way, that way. Nobody else is dancing now, nobody at all . . .

Only her . . .

*

"Amy, this is Ruth. Can you hear me?"

"What? . . . Where?"

"You're in Eddie's car and you've been a bit sick."

Amy tries to lift her head. She changes her mind. It's not a good idea at all to move any bit of her, anywhere.

"We're going to try to get you out of the car and into Terra Firma without waking your dad . . . Amy, can you hear me?"

"Yes," Amy says. Her dress seems to be sticking to her legs. "I can hear you." She opens her eyes. Again, this is not a good idea. She can't see anything and they feel much better closed.

"OK . . . Eddie's going to carry you."

Voices mutter somewhere in the distance.

A car door slams.

Bang.

Like the clap of thunder.

Then everything once again goes a blissfully deep sooty black.

16

Amy hangs over the lavatory bowl and spews into it.

It's not a pretty sight and the smell is worse.

She gets up from her knees and flushes the toilet. Pieces of green sick float around the surface of the water. They remind Amy of the watercress soup she'd longed to throw over Hannah and Dad. Maybe if she'd had the courage to chuck it, Hannah might have disappeared for good, there and then.

She stands shivering, her bare feet on the cold tiles, waiting for the cistern to fill up. It's doing a lot of gurgling. Perhaps it doesn't much enjoy what she's retched into it.

She reaches out for the edge of the handbasin and grips it as hard as she can.

She dares not look at her reflection.

She runs the cold tap until the basin has filled with water. She takes a deep breath, gasping as her face hits the flat icy puddle.

She raises her head.

Jesus! That can't be her in the mirror. The apparition has greenish skin, a lopsided jaw, lank hair and puffy eyes. She hadn't meant to look.

Her head throbs.

She limps to the door, turns off the light, fumbles back across the bathroom, bumps into the bath, stubs her toe, swears, finds the lavatory bowl, flushes the toilet for the second time, flips the seat down and sits on it. She might be sick again.

The cistern is having a field day. Gurgle, churn, slurp, blip. It sounds like the contents of her stomach. Or what remains of them.

Chinks of dawn light filter through the window. A solitary bird begins to cheep.

If I put my head between my knees, maybe the walls will stop spinning.

The door opens. A painfully garish light flashes into her eyes. A long pause hangs in the air, together with the stink of vomit.

"Amy?"

She peers into the voice. It's wearing a long, floaty, smoky-blue nightdress, with deep lacy ruffles around the neck.

"Good *grief*, Amy! What's happened? Are you all right?"

"Hannah." Amy finds it hard to move her lips, so the word comes out sideways. "Never better. What are *you* doing here?"

Hannah ignores the question. Quietly, she closes and locks the door. She moves swiftly towards Amy. In a single swoop, she takes her in her arms.

Amy feels the soft, fragrant nightdress wrapping around her. It's like having Mum again. Hot tears dribble down her cheeks. She mumbles, "I think I must've drunk too much by mistake."

Hannah says firmly, "I know *just* how you feel." She strokes the wet hair out of Amy's eyes. She grabs a handful of tissues and dries Amy's face. She unhooks a bathrobe from behind the door. It belongs to Dad. She lifts Amy to her feet and cuddles her into it.

She whispers, "Come on. Back to bed with you . . . Quietly . . . Don't wake your dad." She unlocks the door. "I'm going to make some tea, and a hot-water bottle, and bring them up to you . . . Quickly now . . . Go and tuck yourself in."

Amy woke to a stone-cold water bottle and the sound of Dora hoovering.

She sat up and groaned. Waves of pain flowed through her head and down her spine. A squalid heap of red silk huddled at the end of the bed.

Someone had wedged a piece of paper on her bedside

table, between the clock and the lamp. She reached for it and held it to her eyes, squinting at it gingerly.

Dear Amy

Hope you had a good sleep and that you're feeling better.

Are you free tomorrow? I've got the day off as it's Saturday. I thought we could go to London together. I need something to wear for the wedding and I'd love to buy you a new outfit too. And shall we have our hair done at somewhere really special?

Give me a ring at the surgery and let me know.

Love

Hannah

From the driveway, Amy could hear Ruth practising.

She opened the door, still holding her beloved violin. She dragged Amy into the hall. "Have you survived?"

"Just about."

"You look a bit peaky."

"You should've seen me at the crack of dawn! . . . Look, about tomorrow."

"Don't tell me. You can't make the concert."

"Would you mind desperately if I didn't? Hannah's offered to buy me an outfit for the wedding."

"Cool!"

"And I felt I couldn't turn her down."

"Where will you go?"

"London . . . Somewhere posh, I expect . . . We probably won't be back till late."

"I think that's *fantastic*."

"We might not find what we want."

"I mean it's brilliant that you're getting on with Hannah."

Amy looked around Ruth's untidy kitchen, at the dishes piled in the sink, the mound of crumpled clothes waiting for the iron. Instead of wanting to clean everything up, Amy suddenly thought the room looked friendly and comfortable.

"Do I have a choice?"

"Give me a ring on Sunday," Ruth said. "I'll come over to inspect your loot."

Amy wallows in a deep tufted chair in a Knightsbridge coffee shop.

Hannah looks at her approvingly. "Your hair's *fabulous*."

"You don't think it's too short?"

"Absolutely not . . . Anyway, it'll grow."

"Yes." Amy sips her cappuccino. "Thanks. It must've cost a bomb."

"Worth every penny. I've only got one maid of honour, haven't I?"

Hannah's crossing things off a complicated list on her organiser. She's left-handed. The sapphire glitters. She says, without looking up, "It's gorgeous, isn't it?"

Amy is silent.

Hannah presses on. "I thought I could wear a kind of blue-green. What do you think?"

Amy remembers Marcello's eyes. "Great."

"Tell you what, let's coordinate our colours. If I wear a slightly darker shade of blue, you could wear a paler one."

"Fine."

"For us, I thought straight dresses with short matching jackets, very simple, but terribly well cut, in a wonderful fabric with a proper lining."

"Sounds good to me."

"And no hats . . . I hate them . . . When I was sixteen, my mother made me wear a tall green creation. I looked like a Christmas tree."

Amy laughs. The sound surprises her. It rings through the coffee shop. There is a sudden hush while people listen.

"I got straight As," she says.

The sapphire stops dead in its tracks. *"What?"*

"My GCSEs. Straight As."

"Amy! That's fantastic! *Another* cause for celebration." Hannah hesitates. "Why didn't William tell me?"

"He doesn't know."

"You mean you haven't *told* him?"

Amy runs her fingers through her new sleek bob. She longs for Chris to see it. She clinches her advantage. "Dad hasn't asked. He's got other things on his mind."

Hannah has the grace to blush.

Over supper that night, as the three of them sat on the terrace, Dad apologised.

He said he'd been a complete idiot to have forgotten about Amy's results. He wanted to take them all out for a slap-up meal next Sunday. Not tomorrow, because there were so many things he and Hannah had to do, but next Sunday was a date. Where would Amy like to go?

Amy sighed. It didn't really matter any more.

He *loved* her new hairstyle. And he quite understood he wasn't allowed to see their new outfits, that Amy had locked hers away and wouldn't even have a dress rehearsal.

The phone rang. Again. It rang incessantly these days, but it was hardly ever for her. It was often for Hannah. Amy wondered irritably why she couldn't use her own mobile . . .

Over the next fortnight Terra Firma began to change its identity.

Wedding presents arrived. Dora stacked them in the living room and the hall and then piled them on the dining-room table.

They ate all their meals in the kitchen.

Hannah's possessions crept into every corner of the house, one by one, as if by magic. Amy would get back to Terra Firma to find a strange coat hanging in the hall, a foreign hand-towel in the downstairs loo, a new painting on the landing wall, a weird-smelling tea in the kitchen, a huge pink toilet bag zipped on the bathroom shelf.

One morning a van arrived. Burly men unloaded two brown-leather armchairs and a wooden chest. Dad said they could take the chairs up to the top floor. The chest was for his bedroom.

Afterwards, Amy checked Mum's study. Her adorable sagging sofa with the squashy Blue Grass cushions had vanished. The chairs sat stiffly in their place.

She raced on to the Common with Tyler, ran until her legs gave way. She'd never forgive Hannah and Dad for dumping Mum's furniture without asking her. Never.

Sweaty and puffing, she sat on a bench, pulled Chris's letter from her pocket. She carried it everywhere, her only crumb of comfort.

Hey, Amy!

How are you? How was the flight home?

We arrived in Rome two days ago and it's blisteringly hot. I'm doing my best to keep up with Jules, whose appetite for all things beautiful seems to increase daily. I must admit mine's starting to flag. I want to see your *beauty more than anything . . .*

We'll soon be home. My agent rang to say he wants me to audition for a small part in a new West End play. He won't tell me what it is, which is infuriating. He says he has his reasons. Something about not reading the lines so often they get stale!

If by any miracle I get the part, it'd be goodbye to Cambridge before I got my degree. It's the last thing in the world my parents want — but then, hey, it's my life, isn't it? My choice.

I think about you all the time. Yesterday I saw a girl who looked so like you I nearly crossed the street and flung my arms around her! I can't wait for the moment when I can do that, once again, with you.

I send you all my love

Christopher

Amy stared at the calendar on her bedroom wall. Tomorrow was the big day. She was terrified. Last night she'd opened the door to Mum's study, only to find Hannah sitting at the desk, checking her wedding list.

"Come in," Hannah sang out. "Plenty of room in here for both of us."

Amy had flung herself out of the room. She slammed the door so hard that Tyler heard the noise from the kitchen and began to wail.

"Sis? It's me."

"Jules! . . . Where are you?"

"On our way home . . . We're going to stop off at Chris's place to pick up his best suit! We should be at Terra Firma by early evening."

"Thank God! It's *chaos* here."

"I bet it is!"

"Everything's happened so *fast*."

"Let's hope they're doing the right thing . . . What time does it all start tomorrow?"

"Register Office at eleven, church blessing midday, back here for a wedding breakfast . . . You'll hardly recognise the house . . . I can't move for flowers, and Tyler's going berserk."

"It'll soon be over, sis."

"Yes." Amy bites the inside of her lip. "Is Chris with you?"

"He's just gone to buy some sandwiches."

"Tell him I can't wait to see him."

"Will do. See you, sis . . . Keep smiling."

"I'll try," Amy says, but when she does, her mouth won't lift into the right shape.

At four o'clock, Amy stops pacing the hall and watching for Christopher.

Suddenly exhausted, she climbs the stairs to Mum's study. Thank God the room is empty. She shuts the door. The stifling air stinks of lily-of-the-valley. Furious, she flings opens a window.

In the garden, someone is testing the fairy lights. They flash on and off like Morse code. Like a warning.

The sky lours, thick with weary cloud, heavy with heat.

After tomorrow, everything will be different.

Hannah will come up here all the time. She'll sit in those disgusting slippery chairs. She'll take over the room. My only real space will be my bedroom. Everything will change.

Something bangs against the door, as if kicking at it.

Amy jumps.

The door flies open.

Dad stands in the doorway, his face white, his eyes blazing.

"Ahhh . . . I thought I might find you here."

"What on earth's the matter?"

Dad doesn't walk towards her. He goes on standing in the doorway, his legs apart, his arms spread wide, as if they are propping up the frame. Like he's doing some silly exercise in his gym.

"You tell me." The words drop like stones. "Shall we start with the name Mrs Baxter?"

"Oh." Amy shivers with shock. She clenches every muscle in her body, trying to keep it taut.

"Yes, *oh*." Dad's voice is louder, heavily sarcastic. "She came to see me this afternoon, at the surgery."

Amy mutters offhandedly, "Didn't know she was one of your patients."

"And guess what she said to me just before she left?"

"Haven't a clue."

Dad snorts with disbelief. "I think you have!"

"Mrs Baxter's a busybody."

"Maybe that's a bloody good thing. She said, 'What a *pity* Amy couldn't come to Paris with us. Is she *better*? We *missed* her. We had *such* a good time.'"

Amy looks at Dad in silence. Lines crinkle the skin around his mouth. His face has turned from white to a peculiar shade of purple. Like a foxglove.

"How d'you think that made me feel, eh? . . . *Have you any idea?*"

Amy likes remaining silent. It gives her time to think.

"Well? What've you got to say for yourself? If you weren't in Paris last month, where the hell *were* you?"

"I didn't go anywhere. I stayed here. I was ill."

"Rubbish. You were fine when Hannah and I left, or we'd never have gone."

"D'you care?"

"Of *course* I care . . . For God's sake, Amy, do we have to go through all this again? You *told* me you'd been to Paris."

"OK, then. I didn't go." She's shaking now, all over, with anger. "So you want to hear the truth?"

Dad shouts, "Don't you think I have the right to know?"

Amy takes a deep breath. Really deep. She fills her lungs so the air in her body will last for the longest possible time. "I went to Fiesole to see Marcello Galanti."

Dad's face is suddenly white again, a yellowy white, blotchy and old. *"Who?"*

"You heard."

"You travelled to *Italy?"*

"Got it in one."

"On your *own?"*

"Yes, Dad . . . Your 'little girl' did something on her own!"

"But . . . why?"

Dad's eyes are beginning to do something weird. They

flicker up and down and from side to side, as if searching for something he cannot find. "Who is this — what did you say his name was?"

Amy screams it to the walls, the ceiling, the heavy, louring sky.

Dad opens his mouth. A blob of spit, like soapsuds, dribbles out of it.

Amy darts across the room. "And don't tell me you've never heard it before, because I won't believe you."

Dad wipes away the spit with his hand. "I don't know what you're talking about."

Amy shoves her face up against his. Right up against it. Really close.

He smells rancid. She knows what he smells of. It is fear.

Suddenly she knows he's guilty as hell.

She whispers, "Yes, you do . . . You're lying."

Dad flinches.

"I think you're a lousy cowardly *liar*."

"How *dare* you!"

She pushes Dad to one side, startled by the depth of her fury, amazed at her strength.

He reels against the door.

One by one the words thrum out of her.

"I'm right, aren't I? My mother's death. You had a hand in it."

Dad gasps as if the words stab him through the heart. He implores her. "Please . . . Amy . . . My darling little girl —"

"Get out of my way."

She is on the landing.

She is racing like a maniac down the stairs.

17

Amy crashes across the hall, through the kitchen and down the garden.

She is out on the Common. She turns right. She doesn't bother to look. She knows exactly where she's going.

She has no air in her lungs to breathe, let alone to run. She slows to a walk, her head down, her legs stiff and full of purpose, as if they are funeral-marching to the stolid beat of a drum.

Left . . . right . . . left . . . right . . . left . . . right . . .

Her trousers brush against her thighs, *swish . . . swish . . .*

The path feels different: she has forgotten how it used to look. It is wilder, more overgrown, more neglected. Massive green ferns with golden tips spill across its edges. Thick tree roots sprawl above the ground, between the stones, tripping her feet.

A sign says: DANGER. NARROW PATHWAY. HORSES STRICTLY FORBIDDEN. It is old and weather-beaten. She's never seen it before. They must have put it up, afterwards.

The Common is swamped in an intolerable humidity. Pleading for a breath of air, Amy cranes her neck to the sky.

A ribbon of lightning cracks silently across it: a huge white crooked finger of admonition from a witch's hand. It sears her eyeballs. She blinks. She can see its livid echo patterning in front of her.

There is silence.

The Common listens and waits.

Then, directly above her, a deafening clap of thunder explodes from the cauldron.

It tears Amy's head apart.

She holds her hands over her ears.

Her legs begin to run, away from the lightning, towards the woods, blindly, swerving, tripping. She can hardly see through the tears, the panting of her breath.

Then something forces her to stop. An invisible barrier she can reach out and almost touch. She lifts her head, wiping at her face.

A gauze curtain, filmy, billowing, seems to float in front of her.

A voice in her head says:

"No entry, Amy.

"No closer.

"This is exactly where it happened.

"So long ago now. So long ago.

"Leave me in peace, my darling child.

"Do not disturb me. Not now. Not ever.

"You have found love. Leave me alone with mine.

"Julian was right, you know. Listen to your brother.

"If you play with fire, it will burn away your heart.

"Leave me in peace, Amy.

"Leave me to die."

Amy's breath chokes into her lungs. She says:

"No, Mum. I need to remember.

"I can't live a moment longer without knowing.

"I'll stand up to it, whatever it is.

"I'm not a child any longer. I'm nobody's little girl.

"Let me learn the truth now.

"Give me back my memory."

Amy raises the palms of her hands.

They tingle with fear.

She uses them to push through the curtain.

She stands the other side of the line.

It is starting to snow again.

Frosty fingers of ice glitter on the gorse. Under the thin sun, they had just begun to melt. Now fresh flakes hang in the sky. They come drifting down, to find a home.

In minutes the path is white, smothered, anonymous.

Cadence whinnies and shakes her head. Snowflakes fly around her ears. Tyler barks for joy. Amy laughs. She tilts her face to the sky, opens her mouth and sticks out her tongue. The snow tastes fresh and clean.

"Watch where you're going, Amy," Mum says.

Amy smiles across at her. Mum's cheeks glow in the cold. Her hair, braided and beautiful, coils beneath her riding cap on the nape of her neck with a serpent's grace.

She smiles back. Duchess's hooves scrape muffled in the snow.

Tyler barks more loudly. He scampers ahead of Amy and shoots into the wood.

Amy calls, "Here, Tyler, here! *Bad* dog."

Mum laughs. The sound rings out in the frosty air. "He's seen the fox, darling . . . You'd better ride after him, or he'll never come out."

Amy and Cadence turn into the wood, under the giant pines.

"Mind how you go," Mum calls. "And don't be long."

The ground is almost dry, soft to the hoof.

Carpets of needles cushion their ride, dulling the pony's trot.

"Tyler!" Amy's voice echoes against the slender trunks of the trees.

There is no welcoming bark.

She rides further, deeper into the wood. "Tyler! Come on now. Come back this minute. Do you hear?"

There is no welcoming bark.

Instead she hears a cry. A woman's voice. A single shriek for help.

It is Mum.

Amy tugs at Cadence's reins. The pony grinds to a standstill. Amy turns her round. Tyler comes flying towards them. Amy gallops out of the wood.

Mum lies sprawled across the path.

Duchess is neighing, skittering around her, crazy with fear.

Amy flings herself off Cadence. She races towards Mum.

Another rider has been here. He has galloped past. Amy can see the tracks. She looks up, terrified. He is riding back to find her, his face is heavy with rage. He is crouched over a powerful black stallion.

Amy knows the horse. He is Marathon. He towers over them.

The rider sees Amy and she meets his eyes.

He gasps, reins in his stallion, turns and gallops off.

Amy bends over Mum.

A jagged boulder lies beneath her head. Her mother's face is pale as the dawn. Blood gushes from her forehead, spurts from her open mouth. She stares wildly at Amy. Her eyes glint like marbles, swirly and round, pale greeny-grey.

"Mum?" Amy touches her shoulder. And more loudly, "Mum!"

The lips begin to move but no words come.

The lips are blue.

Then they are still, and frozen as the snow.

Amy cannot look any longer.

She stands up. Her legs give way. She kneels in the snow, shaking with cold and shock. The rider may return. If he does, maybe he will kill her too.

She scrabbles to her feet. She starts to run. *Anywhere. Fetch help. Find somebody. Tell them to find Mum. To wake her up. She can't be dead. Not like that. Not so fast.*

Someone help me bring her safely home.

Tyler is flying round Mum, barking, pawing the ground, looking at Amy, looking wildly at Mum. Amy tries to call him but the words do not arrive. They are stuck in her throat, lodged within her head. She cannot unlock them, however hard she tries . . .

It begins to rain.

Thick drops splosh on the back of Amy's neck. She sits in the hedgerow, among the wild roses, staring at her clenched hands. Her trousers are snagged with thorns.

Somebody stands beside her. Amy does not bother to look up.

"You were there," she says. "Mum fell off Duchess but you were there. You did nothing to help. You left me there too. In all the blood and snow. You left me there."

"Yes," says her father. "God help me. So I did."

Amy says, "I'm going to the police. All these years you've pretended you had flu . . . "

"I wasn't pretending. I was sick. Really sick."

"That's for sure."

"I meant —"

Amy looks up at him. "I don't care about you any more."

Her father crouches beside her. She can smell him. She wants to push him aside and run away.

"Listen to me. Please. I want to tell you what happened."

"Save it for the police."

"Please, Amy. Listen. Then you can decide what to do."

Amy drops her head between her knees. "What have you got to tell me that I don't already know?"

"You had a baby sister," Dad says. "She died."

The wooden cradle in the shed. Mum weeping in the hammock. Once I found some baby clothes in a drawer. I thought they'd belonged to me. Aunt Charlotte said something to me about women who had too many babies . . .

"Mum had a miscarriage. You were only four. Too young to tell you anything."

Dad is crying now, though he doesn't seem to notice and she couldn't care less.

"We called the baby Elinor. She was the end of our marriage." Dad's eyes are red and raw. "Oh, we stayed together. There was no question of a separation. Nothing like that. But Mum wouldn't let me near her, not then, not ever again.

"When it happened, the miscarriage, I was at a patient's funeral. Mum was on her own. By the time I got to her, she was in hospital – and it was all over and done with.

"I'd always been her doctor. Up till then. Afterwards, everything changed. We never slept together. We never told

Julian, we never told you. We never spoke about it. Mum buried Elinor in her heart and not a word was said.

"Mum wrote two books in three years. We never quarrelled. We never even argued. We just froze together in a terrible politeness."

And I told Ruth they had a perfect marriage . . .

"The morning of the accident, I'd been at work. I'd felt ill for weeks. We had an epidemic. I kept going, head down, because I had to. I'd seen a patient and I blacked out at my desk. Our nurse sent me home. I had a roaring temperature. My body ached as if I had the plague."

"Go on."

"I parked the car and fell into the house. There were letters in the hall. I thought they were for me. Through sheer force of habit, I picked them up, started thumbing through them, not looking, just checking . . .

"I wish to God I hadn't."

He swallowed. Amy glanced at him. She saw Dad's throat working with the effort it took to talk.

"What did you find?"

"They weren't incoming letters. They were bills Mum had paid, letters she'd written, waiting to be posted. The one at the bottom was thicker than the others. It was in a pale-blue airmail envelope. It was addressed to Marcello Galanti."

It felt odd to hear her father say the name.

"I opened it." He held up his hands as Amy started to protest. "I know . . . It wasn't mine to read. But I had a terrible feeling about it. Before I could give myself time to think, I'd ripped it open."

"Was it a love letter?"

"I guess you could say that." Dad's voice changed to a kind of singsong. "Mum said she'd never loved anyone the way she loved Marcello. But that she'd changed her mind. She was cancelling all their plans. She couldn't come to live with him. She couldn't bring you with her. She felt 'obliged' to me for looking after her – and she couldn't leave Julian."

"What else?"

"She wanted Marcello to publish their book. She'd send him permission to do so in a separate document. The Villa Galanti would live in her heart for ever, but Terra Firma and her garden were her home." He bent his head. "She wanted their affair to continue. She could not, she *would* not, give him up."

I'm not surprised. How could anyone give up Marcello?

"How did you feel?"

"Blind rage. I took the letter into the living room and threw it on the fire. I watched it burn. I prodded it with the poker as if it *were* Marcello. I ran out to the stables and threw myself on Marathon.

"I knew the route Mum would have taken . . . It never occurred to me you'd be with her. I thought Cadence was in the stables, that it was your first morning back at school." Dad twisted his body towards her. "I never meant to harm Mum. I just wanted to see her, talk to her, understand what had happened. She'd never said a word to me about Marcello, not a single word. How could I forgive her for *that*?

"I rode like a crazy thing out of the stables. It had begun to snow again. I cursed and swore and rode on. Marathon didn't much like it but I didn't care.

"I heard someone laugh. Lauren's laugh. I galloped round a corner. There she was, on Duchess, *laughing*. Beautiful, joyful — and laughing.

"I saw red. I flew towards her. Lauren saw me coming. In that instant, she knew I'd found out about what she'd been up to. I got closer. When I reached her, she raised her hands to her face, as if she thought I'd lash out.

"I didn't. I never touched her. I hadn't touched her in years. But at that moment, I felt I never wanted to see her again. I wanted her dead. If that's being guilty, then I'm a guilty man.

"I thundered past her. I was *glad* she was scared. I relished it. When I looked back, Duchess had slipped and Lauren fell with her. She cried out. That terrible cry. It haunted me for years. I knew she must've been hurt. I never thought she'd *die*. I galloped on. Then I thought: I can't leave her lying there. I turned Marathon and galloped back. That's when I saw you running from the woods.

"I couldn't believe it. Where had you sprung from, with your red pompom hat and furry gloves? I couldn't face you. I felt so guilty, so sick, so mad with rage. I knew if I didn't get myself into bed, I'd collapse into the snow. So I galloped home."

"You might've saved her if you'd stayed."

"I pushed Marathon into the stables —"

"You're a *doctor*!"

"I was *sick*! I threw myself indoors and into bed. Something in me wanted to die too. I made myself live. For you. For you and Julian."

He reached out for her. She clenched her fists against him. "But the *accident*?"

"I prayed," he said. "Every night. Please, dear God, may Amy never remember."

18

Amy heaves her body to its feet.

It is raining heavily. The trees sigh with relief. Rivulets of water bubble down the path, crawl between the stones.

Amy is soaked. Her hair hangs flat against her neck, her shirt clings to her breasts.

Her father says, "Where are you going?"

She looks down at him. He squats in the hedgerow like a giant toad.

"Terra Firma. I believe that's where I live."

"Amy?"

"What?"

"What are you going to do?"

"I've no idea . . . Think . . . Smile and be polite."

"But — "

"We have guests. Jules and Chris. They'll be waiting at the house."

"But — "

Amy screams, "But what? What do you *want* from me?"

There is a terrible long quiet moment.

Her father says, "Forgiveness."

"Wow! That's a *very* big word!"

"Yes. So is compassion. And understanding." He struggles to his feet. "Please."

Father and daughter face each other in the pouring rain, across the river path. "You must believe me. It was an accident. A terrible mistake."

Amy says, "Shut up! Just shut up and get out of my life!"

"But my *darling* little girl . . . "

"Don't *ever* call me that again." She feels like spitting in his face. "Crawl under a stone. That's where you belong."

She turned and walked away.

She did not look back. She could hear her father behind her, the squelch of his shoes, the sharp intake of his breath. She kept up the ruthless pace, though she knew he was flagging. She could feel his exhaustion but she steeled her heart.

She raced ahead of him.

Knowledge is power . . . I feel powerful . . . A different person . . . I feel whole again. Whatever I decide to do, I've managed to remember my bit of what happened.

That's what matters.

I'll have to believe my father's told me the truth, just like I had to believe Marcello.

And now I must decide what I'm going to do . . .

*

Amy dashed into the house.

She glanced at the note from Hannah on the kitchen table:

Darling, Where are you? I've gone back to my flat to make myself beautiful for tomorrow. Ring me tonight. Sweet dreams. Love you the most. Hannah

Amy clawed at the piece of paper with her wet hands, tore it to shreds and threw it in the bin. She emptied the teapot over it, squashing the tea leaves into a dark stain, wishing Hannah's face lay beneath: just like her father had wanted Marcello to lie under his poker, prodding at the letter in the fire.

She snapped the lid shut and dripped her way into the hall. Jules's and Chris's bags sat on the stairs. She pushed at the living-room door, poked her head around it.

Chris stood up. "Hi!" His eyes had a dazzling light to them.

Amy blew him a kiss.

Jules said, "Sis! . . . Where *have* you been? Talk about a drowned rat!"

Dad stood at Amy's elbow, his breath heaving. "Julian! Christopher! Welcome home! My fault she's so wet!"

Amy moved away from him.

"Dad and I," she said, her voice heavy with sarcasm, "we've been having a little father-and-daughter chat. Before his big day and all." She looked him squarely in the eyes, seeing in front of her a very frightened man. "Haven't we, *Dad?*"

"That's . . . that's right."

"Jules and Chris and I," Amy said casually, "we had *such* a wonderful time in Florence . . . Didn't we, Jules?"

Her brother looked startled and then alarmed.

Dad's mouth dropped open. "What d'you mean?"

"Oh, it wasn't *planned*. You could say we met by *accident*."

Her father's face paled. "How very nice," he squeaked.

"And now," Amy grinned at the three men in her life, "would you excuse me? I simply *must* get out of these wet clothes before I catch my death."

They ate supper in the kitchen.

Julian cooked rice with wild mushrooms. Amy made a salad. Dad and Chris stood around and drank white wine. Dad swallowed half a bottle very fast and opened a second. Julian carved a cooked chicken, cold, straight from the fridge.

Everything tasted like soap.

Amy sat next to Chris. They didn't say much to each other, but every so often Chris's foot would gently nudge hers. Tyler took a shine to Chris and squashed adoringly against his legs.

Nobody mentioned Florence. When the conversation flagged, Julian brayed on about Rome. Dad got steadily drunk.

At the cheese and biscuits stage, Amy stood up. "Would you all excuse me again?"

"Where are you off to?" Her father's eyes flickered warily over her.

"There's something I need to do."

"I hope you're not going *out* this time of night?"

Amy ignored him. She looked at Julian. "You can clear up, can't you? I won't be a minute." She turned at the door. "In fact, you'll hardly notice I'm gone."

She pounded up to her room, sat at her desk, scrabbled between the files for the thick, creamy notepaper with its sepia crest. She read its handwriting three times. Then swiftly, decisively, she wrote:

Dear Marcello

I'm sorry to have taken so long to answer your letter. My father is getting married again. The ceremony is planned for tomorrow. So we've all been very busy at Terra Firma getting ready for the big day.

I've spent a lot of time thinking about you and the Villa Galanti. And about your book in the chapel. I now know that my mother wanted you to publish it.

I'd like to come back to Fiesole. I want to see you again. To read the book. To persuade you to publish it.

Amy Grant

Her heart thumping with impatience, Amy wheeled her bicycle out of the garage.

The road stretched shiny with rain, thick with wet leaves; the sky black, without moon or stars. She flicked on the bike's front and back lights and cycled to the post box. The letter thudded irrevocably into its mouth.

One down . . . Two more to go . . .

She changed direction and set off for Grayshott village. For the small, friendly police house, where she hoped their police officer, Philip Bradley, would be waiting.

She rings the bell.

A light flicks on in the hall. The door opens. Philip peers out.

"Hello! Isn't it Amy Grant?"

"It is."

"Good *evening*! This *is* a nice surprise!"

"Is it?"

"I don't often get calls from you this time of night. Come to think of it, I don't get calls from you at all!"

"No." Amy swallows. "Things have changed . . . There's something you need to know . . . "

Get on with it!

"I've something to tell you."

"Would you like to come in?"

"No." Amy takes a deep breath. "This won't take long."

Philip settles into his listening position: head on one side, eyes wide, arms folded across his policeman's shirt, fingers thrumming.

"It's about my father . . . It's him I've come about."

"Dr Grant?" Philip's eyes light up. "*Such* a lovely man! When my sister was dying, Dr Grant sat with her all night long. Aren't many doctors you can say *that* about."

"You don't understand," Amy says wildly. "My father isn't what he seems."

"How d'you mean?"

"My father," Amy says slowly. "The accident. When my mother died."

"Ah, yes. That *was* unfortunate."

"He kkk . . . " The verb sticks in her throat. She tries again. "He's a mmm —"

The telephone peals in Philip's office. "Would you excuse me a minute? I'll be right back." He trots off.

Amy kicks the doorstep. She hops up and down. She flicks at her hair and hugs her body. The night air smells thick with early autumn.

Philip pops his head round the office door. "Got an emergency on my hands . . . Would you like to come back in the morning?"

"But my father's getting *married* in the morning."

"I see." Philip grins. "*That's* what you've come about."

Amy grabs her bike and wobbles furiously down the road.

The lights are on in Hannah's flat. She leaves the bike sprawled across the pavement, thunders on Hannah's door.

"Who is it?"

"It's Amy . . . Let me in!"

Hannah opens the door. Her hair is smeared with conditioner, her face covered in mud pack. "Amy? This is *not* a good time to call!"

Amy pushes past her. "Good time, bad time, what the hell does it matter?"

"I *beg* your pardon?"

"I've remembered everything." Amy clenches her fists, screws up her eyes, bites her lip. "Every single bloody little moment."

A silence hangs between them.

Hannah sighs. "Ahhh . . . I *see* what this is about." She draws her robe more tightly around her. "You'd better come in and sit down."

Amy flings herself into a chair. She looks up at Hannah. "It was my father on the Common that morning. It was him."

Hannah slides gracefully on to the sofa. "I know."

"What?"

"He told me everything. When we were in Wales. When he asked me to marry him. I know the whole story."

Amy scrambles to her feet. "I don't believe it. You mean, *you* knew but I didn't?"

"He was only trying to protect you. You'd been traumatised. What good would it have done to go over all that old ground?"

"What *good*!"

"Look, Amy. It was an accident. It's over and done with. There's nothing anyone can do about it, not now, not ever."

Amy wobbles across the room. She stands by Hannah's slim body, seeing the outline of her bare breasts under the robe, her mud-packed face, her gleamy shining hair.

"I hate you," she says.

Hannah flinches.

"I won't be at your wedding tomorrow. I don't want to see you again. You can *have* my father. I hope you both rot in hell."

She marches out of the room and down the hall.

Hannah calls, "Wait! Amy, please, don't leave like this."

Amy slams the door behind her and races for her bike.

She throws it back in the garage. It hits the trampoline, shudders to a halt.

Inside the house, Tyler barks.

Dad says, "Ahh, Amy . . . You *did* go out."

Julian flings an arm round Dad's shoulders. "I'm taking Dad for a quiet drink . . . An orange juice. He's already got through several bottles of wine." He looks pointedly at Amy. "This is supposed to be his stag night, after all."

"Thass's sright. S'my *thstag* night . . . Here's to all thstags."

Amy looks at Chris. "That's fine by me."

Dad holds on to Julian. "You can keep Chrisss entertained fra while, can't you, my darlin' liddle gurl?"

"Oh, yes." Amy slips off her coat. "I can do *that* all right."

*

The door slams.

Julian's car drives away.

Tyler curls into his basket and snuffles into sleep.

Chris leaps across the hall.

He takes Amy in his arms.

Amy clings to him, to his gentle, comforting warmth.

Tears begin to rack her body.

They catch in her throat and sting her eyes.

They taste dark as the starless night.

19

They were still talking on the sofa, an hour later, when Julian's car pulled up.

They listened as he helped Dad up the stairs.

"Juss wanna thay goo'night to mah darlin' liddle gurl," Dad growled.

"No, you don't." Julian's voice was firm. "You let her sleep."

Doors banged, taps ran, the cistern grumbled and died.

Amy whispered, "I should go up to bed."

"Not yet." Chris stroked her hair from her forehead, took her once again in his arms. "Not quite yet, my darling little girl."

She sleeps.

Not an ordinary sleep, but one free at last from the nightmares of her mind.

When she wakes it is dawn. She pulls on a tracksuit, slips down the stairs and out into the cool grey air.

As she cycles down the lanes, fog sucks in spirals from the

grass. She hears the creak of her pedals, the insistent purring of wood doves, her own panting, impatient breath.

She rounds the corner to the farm. Golden calves sleep in the field, their tails twitching. She can smell the horses, sees them standing, watching her, in the fields beyond.

She leaps over the metal gate into the stable yard, hears herself call, "Cadence? Cadence, I'm back. I am here for you."

As she runs, she remembers: her mother's laugh, Mary's welcome, the dappled coat and silver mane of her first and only.

On the way back to Terra Firma, Amy stopped at Ruth's.

She hung on the doorbell, woke everybody up, talked to Ruth for a few moments alone in her room.

Then she cycled home.

At eight o'clock she opened her wardrobe.

She took out the dress and the jacket; the shoes and the bag. She lay in a deep bath and washed her hair. She ran down to the kitchen in her bathrobe; fed Tyler; made tea and toast.

Her father called, "Good morning," but she did not answer him.

She ran back to her room. She dried her hair, put on lipstick, slid swiftly into her underwear and then the dress;

the shoes and then the jacket. She filled her bag. She looked at herself in the mirror.

Yes, she would do.

She sat at her desk and wrote:

Dad, I can't come to the Register Office. I don't want to see you marry Hannah. I'm sure you'll understand why. Chris and Jules are still asleep. Please tell them for me.

I'll wait for you in the churchyard. I have things to say to you, things we must discuss, before the blessing. If you don't agree to what I want to do, I shall not attend the blessing and I shall never see you again.

Amy

She pushed the note under her father's door and walked out of the house.

Amy shivers.

The dress is short and the jacket barely touches her waist. Her hands are freezing and the wedding party are late. She paces around the churchyard. The shoes have high heels and she cannot move all that fast. The odd passer-by stares at her and wanders on.

The cars start to arrive. Her father gets out of the first.

He is wearing a pale-grey suit and an embroidered blue waistcoat. He has slicked his hair back from his forehead but Amy knows it isn't going to stay like that. Not for long.

She sits on the bench and waits.

"You look beautiful," he says.

"Thanks."

He holds out his hand. "Hannah and I are married."

She looks at the wedding ring, biting into his flesh. "So I see."

"Thank you for letting me —"

"Sit down. There are things I need to say."

"Of course . . . Anything."

Amy swallows. "I know it was an accident."

He drops his head into his hands. "Thank God."

"But the fact you never told me the truth — and that you left Mum lying there — I think that was despicable. I can never feel the same way about you. But you're my father and I want you to get on with your life. As best you can."

"Thank you."

"I shan't tell Jules and I shan't tell Chris. I shan't tell anyone." Amy smiles wryly. "It'll be our little secret." She clenches her fists. "But in return you must agree to what I want to do."

"*Anything.*"

Amy stands up. "I've written to Marcello."

"*What?*"

"I posted the letter last night."

"So *that's* where you —"

"Yes." Amy stares at the gravestones, at the way they heave from the ground. "I've told him I want to go back to the Villa Galanti. To read the book. His and Mum's book. I want him to publish it . . . It's what Mum wanted . . . I think we should honour that request."

Her father is crying now; his body racks with sobs.

"If you want me to be your maid of honour you will have to say yes."

"Yes," her father moans. "Yes, of course . . . What else can I say?"

"Good." She opens her bag and gives him her handkerchief. "Here. Wipe your face and pull yourself together."

He blows his nose. It sounds like a trumpet singing over the graves of the dead.

"This morning, very early, I did something else." Amy bites her lip. "I went to find Cadence . . . She's just the same as ever. Just as beautiful. I rode her down the lanes. It was wonderful."

Her father's face glitters through his tears. "Can we —"

"Yes. I want us to open the stables. I want to ride again."

Dad stumbles to his feet.

"No, don't touch me." She turns away from him. "I've got something else I need to do . . . Go and find your wife."

Amy walks, slowly, into the centre of the yard of graves.

Crunch, punch snap the stones beneath her heels. An autumn wasp zooms viciously against her cheek.

Her mother's gravestone winks up at her from waves of grass that nobody has cut. The granite shimmers in the light, grey flecked with black. Amy bends towards it. The sleeves of her jacket rustle against her arms.

She strokes her fingers over the edge of the stone. Its roughness bites. She gasps. The granite has drawn blood. She opens her mouth and coughs. Fluid rises from her lungs. She swallows it down again.

"I've come to say 'hello'," Amy says.

She recites the words to herself, as if she is learning how to read:

In memory of Lauren Grant
Wife to William
Mother to Amy and Julian
Sister to Charlotte
We who live on will always love you

"I'm going back to Fiesole."

Amy fights back the tears but loses the battle. She straightens her back.

"And then I'll come to talk to you again."

In the church there are flowers and music, crowds of heads and hats, the scent of lavender.

Dad and Hannah try to smile at her. They turn and start to walk down the aisle.

Amy hesitates.

She stares at the flagged floor.

She longs to back away, to race out of the church, out of the village, on and on, into the wind and the sun, until she reaches nowhere.

She raises her head.

In front of her, holding her garden in her arms, glimmers the stained-glass image of Saint Elizabeth.

Amy hears Mum's voice: *What I love about her is her strength . . .*

She bows her head, willing herself to move.

Slowly, stiffly, with all eyes upon her, she walks down the aisle.

She moves towards Christopher's side and slips her hand in his.